FPL
Y

THIRTEEN
DAYS TO
MIDNIGHT

THIRTEEN DAYS TO MIDNIGHT

PATRICK CARMAN

(L)(B)

LITTLE, BROWN AND COMPANY

New York · Boston

Little, Brown and Company

Hachette Book Group
237 Park Avenue, New York, NY 10017
Visit our website at www.lb-teens.com

Little, Brown and Company is a division of Hachette Book Group, Inc.
The Little, Brown name and logo are trademarks of Hachette Book Group, Inc.

First Edition: April 2010

978-0-316-00403-9

10 9 8 7 6 5 4 3 2 1

RRD-C

Design by David Caplan
Printed in the United States of America

For Peter Rubie,
friend and mentor

MIDNIGHT

Jacob Fielding stood in a small room and stared at a body. It was a dead body, someone he could have saved but chose not to. Jacob had let the person die because, in his view, it was the right thing to do.

He watched in silence, felt the air in his lungs catch and flutter as he tried to stay calm. What was he going to do now? How could he explain? People wouldn't understand. They'd say he was a killer.

The body hadn't moved in the seven minutes Jacob Fielding stared at it, but it had made some unpleasant sounds that would lodge in his memory and prove difficult to get rid of.

"All of us play the same tune sooner or later," Jacob's best friend said. "The black symphony of the dead."

Milo Coffin with the dyed hair and the dark humor. He of all people would know.

Jacob took out Mr. Fielding's Zippo lighter and flicked it open, searching for a distraction. He heard the clank of metal and the sandpaper jingle of fire coming to life.

He held the flame under his fingers and wished it would burn, but it didn't.

Jacob Fielding had come to believe that death was his closest friend. It was there when he stood in front of the mirror in the morning, there when he wrote and talked and slept. Death was always watching, trying to decide if the time had come to step into the spotlight.

Jacob Fielding was an expert in his field, and death was his subject.

It was the enemy he had come to love.

ONE DAY LATER

If you could have only one superpower, what would it be?

People get that question all the time, but hardly anyone I've asked has a logical answer. I'm surprised by how often people answer flying, because when you really stop to think about it, flying is dangerous as hell. Just figuring out how to do it right would more than likely involve slamming into a building, so you'd probably be dead or badly injured in the first ten minutes. Best-case scenario you'd get some other power to go along with it—like turning into liquid if you hit a slab of pavement doing ninety.

But then, adding something else into the mix is more than the question allows for.

If you could have only *one* superpower, what would it be?

Invisibility has a lot going for it. It's not the sort of super-power that would automatically get you hurt and seriously, there are some sweet ways you could put that kind of talent to good use: girls' locker room, gathering dirt on overbearing teachers, tripping people...But you're not getting invisible clothes to go with your invisibility. Getting used to walking around in the buff 24-7 would be damn hard to do. I'd die of stress just thinking about having my skills fail me while trying to escape from KFC with a bucket of chicken.

And this brings up another huge problem. Temptation.

Say you get lucky and somehow the invisibility power comes with a set of invisible clothes. You'd be on the dark side before you could curl your toes and count to ten. Nobody I hang out with could walk into a Kmart totally invisible and leave without stealing video games, DVDs, and cans of Red Bull up the wazoo. If you can hide it under your invisible jacket, you're taking it. And that's not a super-power, that's a lose-your-soul-to-the-devil power. I should know—I go to a Catholic school and I'm telling you: invisibility = eternal damnation. You can take it to the bank.

Reading minds? That one blows from the word go. Listening to the crap going through the minds of all the idiots at my school all day? No, thanks.

Throwing balls of fire, time travel, nunchuck skills... blah, blah, blah. I've worked my way through every super-power there is and found them all wanting for one reason or another. The truth is that every power, no matter how amazing, is loaded with trouble of the worst kind.

It would have been nice if someone had let me in on the joke thirteen days ago. Things could have been a lot easier for me.

This is how it went down, or at least how I remember it. I don't have a superhuman memory, but I can tell you this much for sure:

I killed a guy, maybe two. Possibly three.

I have one power. Not two or three or four. Just one.

I met a girl, and she changed everything.

THIRTEEN
DAYS TO
MIDNIGHT

8:12 AM
MONDAY, OCTOBER 8TH

I arrived in the parking lot full of cars after the morning bell on purpose, just in case I changed my mind and wanted to cut school after all. It felt like all the blood had been drained out of the world while I was away.

The sky was overcast and heavy. Around here, clouds can take in water for weeks on end, then drizzle for twenty-five or thirty days in a row, slowly delivering back what they've stolen. Looking up, I had the feeling we were in for a long month of misty rain.

Ten out of ten cars in the Holy Cross parking lot were crap for a simple reason: Holy Cross was a dying school. Enrollment had been in a freefall for years, and they'd dwindled to 137 souls in four grades by the time I got there as a gangly, foul-mouthed sophomore. I've since cleaned up my language—mainly because it bothered Mr. Fielding so much—but I still remember the gorgeous sound of a well-placed F-word rolling off my tongue.

Two years ago they finished building South Ridge High, a brand new 1,300-student public high school with state-of-the-art everything. Its high-tech and pristine athletic facilities are housed a mere mile down the road. When that place fired up its lights for the first time, most of the best athletes, brainiacs, and teachers took off. What was left were kids with parents who'd gone to Holy Cross before them in the eighties, back when three hundred kids packed the halls between classes.

Just so we're clear from the beginning, me and my friends *hate* South Ridge High, especially the defectors who used to be Holy Crossers. We're a wad of chewing gum on the heel of mighty South Ridge, and they never let us forget it.

As I stared at the clunkers in the parking lot and felt the oppressively low clouds closing in, school was the last place I felt like spending the day, especially given all that had happened. I was just about to turn around and head for the 7-Eleven when I was spotted by Miss Pines, a mostly pretty, often tired-looking fiction writer who taught second period English and was eternally late for every class.

"Jacob Fielding, nice to have you back," said Miss Pines, flipping shut her cell phone as she kicked her car door shut. Miss Pines, the only black teacher at our school, almost always wore yellow, and today was no exception.

"I was so sorry to hear about Mr. Fielding," she continued.

She was one of the strictest teachers at Holy Cross, but she could be nice when the situation called for it. Miss Pines looked at me sort of sideways, a habit she had that always preceded a question. "How you holding up?"

"Better than this place," I said, only half joking. "How about you?"

"I'm fine. Late as usual, but fine. I got that trait from my mom. She was tardy for everything—church, work, dinner on the table. You know I didn't show up on time for school but three times my whole freshman year? I blame her for all my problems."

"Good thing I don't have that difficulty," I said. "The mom thing, I mean."

"Maybe so," said Miss Pines, nodding thoughtfully as if she really might think this was true. She tilted her head again. "Still expecting Father Tim back tomorrow night?"

"As far as I know."

Holy Cross was in need of cash and it was Father Tim's job to get it, which meant driving from Salem to Seattle to meet with the bishop. In a small school it's tough to keep that sort of thing secret, especially when one of the students (that'd be me) is living in the church house now.

"How's the novel?" I asked. As far as I knew, Miss Pines had been working on the same manuscript for about ten years.

"Same as when you asked me last time. Not finished."

Miss Pines moved on, yelling over her shoulder that she was *really* late, which meant I was late, which meant I'd better get moving.

I lingered in the parking lot a little longer, staring at the countless weeds poking through cracked concrete, thinking about what had kept me away from school for a whole week. Mr. Fielding, my foster parent, was dead. There was no Mrs. Fielding, which complicated matters. And then there was the fact that I loved the guy, and the additional detail about how we were together when it happened— only he died, and I didn't.

I heard two quick taps on a horn, which shook me out of my misery, and knew without looking that Milo was coming up the long driveway in his egg-white Geo Metro. He pulled into an empty spot in front of me and lurched to a stop, got out, slammed the door, and, leaning hard on the rim of the windshield, folded his arms across his chest. He looked me up and down like I was a prowler from South Ridge about to layer the school in graffiti.

"You're not seriously going in there looking like that?"

Glancing down at my school uniform, I saw he had a point. It was pressed to wrinkle-free perfection. Milo slacked on the school dress code wherever legally possible. He'd tried black eyeliner, army boots with missing laces, and a string of ill-advised piercings (ears, nose, eyebrow). In every case, he'd been sent home by Father Tim with the same message: "Not in my school."

"Nice to see you, too, Milo. Glad you missed me."

I dropped my heavy backpack on the wet pavement and began rolling up the white sleeves of my shirt.

"A'right, look—I'll cut you some slack because, you

know, because of everything that's going on. But I'm not the one who went dark for a week. That'd be you." Milo picked at the silver duct tape holding the windshield of his car in place. Rust was winning an all-out assault on both front doors, the trunk was held down with a twisted bungee chord, and both bumpers had fallen off. "And don't tell me you dropped your cell phone in the john again. I'm not buying it. What have you been doing with yourself?"

I loosened my tie a few notches and picked up my bag. There were no lockers at Holy Cross, so the bag was stupidly heavy, loaded down with books and homework I'd not been able to touch for days.

"Well? Are you gonna answer me or do I have to beat it out of you?" asked Milo.

"Go ahead, hit a guy while he's down." I had the excuse of a lifetime for going dark, but I still felt bad for flaming out on my closest friend at Holy Cross.

He'd dug up the corner of the tape and began pulling it with his fingers. "You're beating yourself up pretty good without my help," he mumbled.

I'm quite a bit taller than Milo, but I'm also rail-thin. Milo, on the other hand, is short and solid, a ferocious wrestler. He'd have no problem kicking the crap out of me if he ever wanted to. But right now, he was just trying to pull me back into the land of the living. I got that.

"Sorry, okay? I just needed to be alone. I was on lockdown at the church house, getting my head straight. It actually felt pretty good, being off the grid for a week."

"It's cool." Milo lifted his head as he kicked the gravelly parking lot. "I'm sure it ain't easy. But you can't just disappear like that. People ask about you. They expect me to know something."

"Let 'em wonder. I don't care anymore."

"If you weren't in such bad shape already I'd put the Holy Cross on your grieving head." The "Holy Cross" was like a headlock, only you held the guy in reverse and rapped his forehead with your knuckles. Hell of a move if you could pull it off without getting bitten in the process.

"Don't go easy on me. I'm fine."

"Don't tempt me."

I smiled. Things were back to how they'd always been between us. I'd met Milo first, before anyone else at Holy Cross, at his parents' bookstore. "You ready for this place again?" asked Milo, pushing the long strip of duct tape back in place with the heel of his hand.

"Probably not. But the church house is creepy quiet, especially with Father Tim out of town. He's not coming back until tomorrow night and the old guys are downright depressing. Better here than watching dust collect on Bibles."

A dull silence hung between us. How do you talk to your friend about death and loneliness—and guilt?

Milo's phone vibrated, and he reached into his pocket, reading a text that had just arrived.

"Someone new showed up while you were gone," he said, clicking out a message and returning his phone to his pocket.

"You're kidding. Guy or girl?"

"Girl."

"Promising. What's she look like?"

"You'll see."

Milo pointed into the backseat of his car, and I leaned closer, spotting a red skullcap and a longboard.

"She left her stuff in your backseat?"

"You guessed it."

"She must be a real dog."

"Nope."

I was damn near positive Milo was lying.

"Hang for the morning, and I promise you won't be sorry," said Milo, sensing I was thinking of ditching school for another day of solitary confinement. "I'll introduce you to the new girl. She has something for you."

"She doesn't even know me."

"She knows enough."

Milo started for the entrance to Holy Cross and I weighed my options: enter the school and find a girl with a gift (odds are she'd be hideous if she existed at all), or I could return to the church house and watch retired priests play dominoes and talk about gardening.

I decided to follow Milo into the school.

◆ ◆ ◆

We were already late for first period, so the halls were empty when Milo opened the door to Mr. D's science class and left me standing in the gap. There's nothing quite as unnerving as incoherent mumbling and the sound of phone keys texting the moment you walk into a room.

"Well, everyone knows you're back now," said Milo, moving off toward his own first period class. "At least that's over with. Don't cut out at lunch, I told Ophelia to meet us."

"Ophelia?"

I stood in the doorway listening to the sound of thumbs on little keyboards.

"Text at your own peril," shouted Mr. D, picking a wooden box up off his desk. It was widely known that if your phone ended up in Mr. D's box he would hold it for a week and answer all your incoming messages with the same four words: *shut your pie hole.*

Not bad for an old guy.

Attending a small private school has a certain routine that must be endured. Everyone knows everyone else, and even if we're in different groups or flat-out hate each other, there's a persistent problem that hovers over the school: We're all stuck with one another. I think this is one of the main reasons we lost so many to South Ridge. Over there a guy could pick a new friend every seven minutes and never run out. Not the case at Holy Cross.

And so I tolerated the sympathetic looks of Mr. D and all the guys in the class. I tolerated the half hugs and sweet smiles of Mary, June, Emily, Bethany, Marissa, Madison, and Taylor, who all approached me. And then, mercifully, it was over and Mr. D was telling everyone to settle down and turn to page 215.

I slid into my seat and looked around the room, making sure I hadn't missed a new girl with the face of a cow and long, dark hairs growing out her nose. Whoever Ophelia was, if she was at all, she'd be in the other first period class with Miss Pines. All the faces in Mr. D's class were ones I'd seen before.

Ethan poked me in the back with a pencil.

"Yo, man. Good to have you back. This place sucks without you. Tennis at lunch." It wasn't a question. That's Ethan for you.

"Nah. It started raining."

"Who the hell cares if it's raining?"

Everything is always a competition with Ethan. The only reason he wants to go out in the rain and play tennis is so he can beat me. This is the guy who thinks he's everyone's buddy, thinks he's extremely funny, thinks he's a lot of things everyone just sort of puts up with because he's big, his parents have money, and he's good-looking. Unfortunately, he's also stupid, loud, and ignorant.

"Got plans," I said. "Maybe tomorrow."

"*Psss,*" Ethan scoffed, and I knew without looking he was shaking his head. I set my sights on Mr. D and tried to concentrate.

Probably the thing I like best about Holy Cross is the fact that most of the classes are taught by normal people pretending to be teachers. As long as private schools in

Oregon produce students who pass state tests, they can hire whomever they want. Our science teacher, Mr. D, is also a swing-shift manager at Walmart. Mr. Beck, the social studies teacher, is an emergency plumber. At least twice a week his cell phone rings in the middle of class and he goes into panic mode, like he's just answered the Bat phone. Our math teacher is a seasonal fisherman in Alaska, where he claims to make more money in six weeks than he does all year teaching at Holy Cross.

It seems like every teacher at Holy Cross has something going on the side except Father Tim, who runs the place and teaches religion and philosophy. He's never taken a state teaching exam in his life.

"I'll bet you five bucks. Come on, one game," whispered Ethan.

I shrugged off the pencil sticking into my shoulder blade and raised my hand.

"Mr. D? Ethan keeps mumbling and poking me in the back with his pencil. I think he needs a time out."

Ethan laughed his loud, obnoxious, howler of a laugh — the one you can hear a hallway away — and Mr. D moved him to the front row.

I suffered Ethan in the hallway after class. He wouldn't let up about the match, wouldn't come unglued from my side.

There were two other guys I hung out with once in a while, Nick and Phil, who were kind of like Laurel and Hardy, but less funny. When they walked by, Ethan commented on my lameness and let out a howler. They looked predictably unimpressed.

"You meet the new girl yet?" asked Nick, an overweight, big-headed guy with insane hair.

I shook my head no.

Nick was the largest guy in school and, thank god for all of us, a peacekeeping force. He hated fights. He was also quicker than he looked, a real killer on the court.

"She's unapproachable," Phil commented. "*Totally* unapproachable." Phil's shy as hell. He's got this thin head of red hair that screams *I will be bald at twenty-five.*

"She talks to me plenty," said Ethan.

"Liar," said Nick. He glared at Ethan, who shrugged.

Nick gave Phil's shoulder a shake. "Our man Phil here is saving his A game. Just give him time. Besides, this new girl? She's all into Milo anyway. The two of them are an exclusive club unto themselves."

Phil and Nick drifted down a corridor. Other people hovered like bees, bumped fists, offered condolences. All morning I searched the faces for someone new and came up empty.

When the bell rang right before lunch I bolted for the door before Ethan could catch me and went straight for the spot where Milo and I always ate, out in the courtyard. Holy Cross was built in a square around an open courtyard, which was great in the spring but rotten in the winter. Raindrops snuck in under the covered halls, cold wind whipped across paint-chipped poles holding up the ceiling, and dead leaves were everywhere. There were two stone tables out there with carved benches on either side. It wasn't likely to be popular today, since the rain was a buzz kill.

I saw Milo already waiting for me. Alone.

I started down one of the four pathways into the courtyard, feeling a mist on my cheeks. Shrubs and bushes and small trees lined the pebbled walk. Everything smelled green and damp.

"Not a great place for lunch, Milo, especially since I didn't *bring* a lunch."

"A little rain never hurt anyone. Stop your complaining."

"Gimme a break! It's cheese zombie day. I've been missing those things. Let's go." Cheese zombies = hoagie rolls smothered in melted cheddar.

"Your cheese fix can wait," said Milo.

My stomach rumbled in response. "How'd you end up on the receiving end of this girl's attention, anyway? Sounds like she doesn't talk to anyone else but you."

Milo glanced up at me like I'd discovered a secret or something.

"Hey, what can I say, the chick latched on to me. I had very little to do with it."

"She goth?"

"No."

"She's slumming, that it?"

Milo rolled his eyes, then assumed a wrestler's crouched position, his quick feet dancing back and forth on the gravel. I started laughing.

"If you have to know," said Milo, standing upright again, "I met her downtown at Eddies. First place she came when she arrived in town, a few days before she stepped foot on campus. She keeps to herself and I met her first. What do you want me to say? She's comfortable around me."

Eddies was a thrift store that carried nothing but clothes, mostly black. "This girl went into Eddies? What the hell for?"

"Hey, don't be like that. Eddies is cool."

"It's a freakin' mausoleum. She's goth. Has to be. A goth cow."

I stuffed my hands in my pockets and glanced toward the dry, covered hallway. Phil and Nick were standing together, staring across the courtyard, looking sort of perplexed or... I don't know, mesmerized. I followed their gaze, down the opposite pebbled pathway from which I'd come.

And there she was, like a ghost or an apparition gliding out of the safety of the school.

"So she's real after all," I mumbled, feeling a faint sort of light-headedness at the sight of the girl walking toward us.

"Oh, she's real," said Milo with a wispy sort of laugh. "And like I said, she's got something for you."

◆　◆　◆

"Sign here."

Those were the first words I ever heard Ophelia James say. I watched her as she approached through the hazy courtyard in what felt like slow motion, dropped her

21

backpack on the stone bench next to mine, and sat on it so her butt wouldn't get wet. She was holding out her arm, a pink cast covering it from her hand to her elbow. There wasn't a single signature on it. I was struck silent.

Let me give you a sense of what I was dealing with here.

This girl was, in a word, stunning. Blond hair, and I don't mean the sandy kind. I mean long, straight, creamy-colored California beach blond. It's not very common in my neck of the woods and it caught me completely off guard. Her perfect skin was, as far as I could tell, completely devoid of makeup. Very cute face with one of those slightly upturned noses I just love. And not to be totally Manwich, but Ophelia James had a body that curved perfectly at every point. The only sane reason a heterosexual fifteen-year-old guy would take his eyes off her boobs? To stare at her butt as she was walking away.

But it was her eyes that did it, I think, a light hazel that popped almost unnaturally. And those piercing eyes, they locked on me from the moment I saw her. She stared, holding out her arm.

"Sign here," she repeated.

"Jacob Fielding, meet Ophelia James," said Milo.

Ophelia rolled her eyes and lightly punched Milo in the shoulder. They already seemed super close. Great.

"Just call me Oh, like everyone else does," Oh replied, still giving me that intense stare.

I paused for a half second, broke our mutual gaze with some serious effort, and looked at the bright pink color of a cast without markings. How could anyone, let alone someone this pretty, go even five minutes without getting mauled by guys wanting to sign her cast?

I said the first thing that came to mind and then immediately wished I were a mute boy sucking on a sock.

"Not too popular, I see. That must be rough."

She looked at Milo, clearly amused, and said, "You didn't tell me he was a comedian."

She turned back and gave me a much more resolved look. It was a look I would come to know well in the thirteen days that followed.

"Milo told me about your foster dad. I figured it must be tough for you right now, so first place on a hot pink cast seemed like the least I could do. But if you want, I can let Phil sign it first."

We all looked toward Phil. He'd have a heart attack if Ophelia James so much as talked to him.

"Let's move this meeting to my car," said Milo, wiping the rain from his forehead.

"Can we stop at the cafeteria?" asked Ophelia. "I'm starting to crave a cheese bomb."

"Since I blew my opening line, I'll get the food," I said, trying not to sound desperate despite feeling like I'd swallowed my tongue. "You guys go ahead, I'll meet you."

Five minutes later we were all sitting in Milo's car—he and Ophelia in the front seat, me in the back. The windows were fogged, hiding us from anyone outside, and our zombies steamed in the sticky air.

"I freakin' love these things," she said between mouthfuls of cheese.

"Close call," said Milo. "You know Jacob here swore off swearing at the start of the school year."

"You're *kidding*," said Ophelia, eyes darting between me and Milo.

"Nope," said Milo. "Certain four-letter words repel him, so I'm told."

I laughed and felt like I was very close to shooting cheese up my nose.

"I'm not that serious about it," I said.

"Are too," said Milo.

I rolled my eyes and took another bite.

"Say the F-word," said Ophelia. She was drilling down on me with those hazel eyes and this very thin, wry smile that I loved.

"Can't do it," I said. "I've got a streak going. Ninety-six days. If I hit a hundred, maybe I'll reward myself."

"I can respect that."

Milo let fly a string of cheese-laced profanities a mile long and we all laughed until we cried. There were words and phrases in there I couldn't even begin to say in front of a pretty girl.

When we calmed down, I tried to explain.

"It wasn't a big deal," I said. "Until after the, you know, after it happened."

Stupid move. Never bring up the death of someone close to you as a conversation starter. It's worse than talking about your old girlfriend. Ophelia looked at Milo uncomfortably.

"Look, you guys, it's okay," I started again. "I'm just saying, Mr. Fielding asked me to stop cursing all the time and at first it was like, who, me? But then I started listening to myself—this was like four months ago—and he was right. And since he's gone now, I don't know, I figure I can keep it going a little while longer."

"I think it's sweet," said Ophelia, again with those eyes and the upturned corner of her mouth. It was heaven.

Ophelia unzipped her backpack and pulled out a brand-new Sharpie.

"It's now or never," she said, holding the perfect pink cast out to me.

I took the pen and felt a sudden panic about what I would write. All that time walking to the cafeteria and back and for some reason I hadn't thought about what I would do if I got the pen in my hand. I stalled.

"How do you spell your name? O-P-H…"

"Just Oh. O-H."

"How'd you break it?" I asked.

"Oh come on, just sign the damn thing and let's get outta here," said Milo. "The bell's about to go off."

"It's my third break in two years," said Oh, lifting her chin in the direction of her longboard propped up next to me in the backseat. "Concrete surfing, gets me every time."

"I can respect *that*," I said. Smooth, Jacob. I think Milo actually winced.

25

All I could think about was what Oh would want me to write. I wanted her to think I was a smart, funny future husband and father of her many children.

And then it came to me, like a lightning bolt out of nowhere, the words were there and I wrote them, big and bold all across the best real estate on Oh's perfect pink cast.

You are indestructible. ♪

For some reason I felt light-headed when I finished writing and looked up at her, like I'd stood up too fast or the oxygen had left my brain. Oh pulled her arm back, looked thoughtfully at the words, and replied, "It's upside down, but I like it. You done good, Jacob."

I gave Oh back her pen and we got out of Milo's clunker at the sound of the bell. The words I'd written were strangely appropriate for a cast, like a well-timed joke, but also a protective gesture, a nice sentiment for a girl who keeps falling down.

You are indestructible.

The thing was, I'd stolen the sentiment. They were the last words Mr. Fielding ever said to me, and I'd tossed those last words off as an opening line to a pretty girl. What the hell was wrong with me?

You are indestructible.

Those were the last words I heard before we hit the wide, moss-covered trunk of an old-growth tree in Mr. Fielding's car doing sixty.

FIFTEEN YEARS IN FIVE MINUTES FLAT

There's a lot to tell about the past thirteen days, so I'm not going to squander too much time on the fifteen years that came before.

All I know about my dad is that he was in prison when I was born and that he died of an overdose when I was two. He never saw me, I never saw him. I do have a sort of half-vision of my mother that's all grainy and torn up. One of my earliest memories is me with an ice-cream cone, standing on a street corner in downtown Portland. Someone took my sticky hand and I began walking. I remember the taste of the ice cream and how my fingers were shaking. When I looked up into the blue sky there was a face staring down at me, but it wasn't my mother. And...that's pretty much it. To this day, whenever I eat ice cream, my fingers shake uncontrollably.

That ice-cream cone marked the beginning of my career as a boarder in the Oregon foster care system. No one ever adopted me. Four-year-old boys are a tough sell. Five, six, and seven are even tougher. Eight and above is just shy of statistically impossible, like winning the lottery. At some point along the way, around ten years old, I accepted the idea that I wasn't ever going to have a family.

Some of the places I stayed were pretty good, some of them not great, and one was pretty bad. When I was eleven, I roomed with a kid whose parents were junkies drifting in and out of prison. I hate to say it, but that kid was trouble. I used to run away when I saw him coming. He was in a rage all the time.

Ever since then, running became a weird habit of mine. Over the years, if I saw something that made me nervous or gave me a bad feeling in the pit of my gut, I turned and ran. I mean I *actually* started running in the opposite direction. Maybe that's why I didn't get in a lot of trouble, I don't know.

The last foster home I stayed in was run by an overweight lady by the name of Joanne who traded foster kids like baseball cards. With Joanne, you were in a line of six teenagers and when you'd been there the longest, it was your turn to go. She wore the same gunnysack-shaped dresses every day, all in varying shades of blue, with two exceptions: black gunnysack when someone was leaving, red when someone new was showing up. When I'd seen five red dresses, I knew my days were numbered at Joanne's.

Joanne had this other ritual about letting kids go. She took care of all the details ahead of time, then packed everyone but the person leaving into her Suburban and left for the day in her black dress. Coming back was always strange, because someone was gone and you might not see them ever again. Sometimes it felt like they'd never been there to begin with.

I have to admit, when the time came for me to go, I was glad to be standing all alone on the gravel driveway. It was easier that way. At that point I was pretty sure I'd never find a place that felt permanent.

I met Mr. Fielding about sixteen months ago. He belonged in Oregon the way a trout belongs in Montana. He was probably fifty...or forty...or sixty. It was hard to tell, and he refused to say how old he was, enjoying the fact that I couldn't settle on a number.

I guess the best way I could describe Mr. Fielding at first sight was that he was a man's man, and like some part of him had been lost or was lonely. From underneath a tattered Mariners baseball cap, he had a good three inches of dark hair that looked like tangled wire. There was a gap in his front teeth when he smiled, a kind of shy smile that even I couldn't be suspicious of—after fifteen years of learning to be suspicious of *everyone*. Bright blue eyes, a thin layer of facial hair, sideburns I would've died for. He wore a rugged sort of wool shirt, a pair of Dickies work pants, and boots that might have been older than he was. He smelled of pipe tobacco.

He came all the way from Salem to pick me up. I'd never been out of Portland until then, and even though Salem was only an hour away, to me it felt like Mr. Fielding had heard I was available and come from the other side of the universe to find me.

I'll never forget his first words to me. "You wouldn't by any chance be a connoisseur of the perfect breakfast?"

I kicked the gravel with the toe of my tennis shoe, tried to act uninterested even though I was starving.

"I might be," I answered, all attitude at the sight of this overgrown granola head. "Why you ask?"

He looked at the red house behind me and the field of weeds farther still, smelling the air the way a man of the outdoors smells the air, with curiosity.

"If you can get me to Northwest Glisan, and you're the least bit hungry, I believe you'll be pleased."

My stomach won out, and we drove in the opposite direction of Salem in order to find an obscure little restaurant called the Tin Shed. This would later become one of our great habits together: Saturday morning, in the car, in search of huevos rancheros, biscuits and gravy, coffee to die for, anything baked and smothered in butter. More often than not we drove for over an hour to find something new we'd heard about.

Those drives in the car became like a ritual. Stuck with each other in search of the Cadillac Café, the Long Branch, Gravy's, Cory Miners, Mother's Bistro, and dozens of other breakfast meccas, there was nothing to do but get to know each other, mile by mile. We talked about food, the weather, sports, comic books, sci-fi novels, movies. We ate copious amounts of bacon, pancakes, waffles, omelets, and downed it all with cup after cup of strong coffee.

It was damn nice, no other way to say it. Just damn nice.

I miss the car rides, the smell of breakfast, the paper, the nothing on the surface sort of chitchat that somehow added up to so much by the time the waitress cleared the plates. We were both far too late to the game to become father and son. We were friends. And that, as it turned out, was enough.

I ended up at Holy Cross because of a conversation on the way to Gravy's in Portland. The summer was about up. Three more weeks and I would start school in Salem. I was sure I'd be attending South Ridge like four hundred or so other freshmen.

It began with a surprising question from Mr. Fielding, as so many of our conversations did.

"Have you got any ideas about the Catholics?"

I took a deep breath and thought for a second. What did I know about Catholics?

"They invented the Pope. And racquetball. They've been around a while. How am I doing?"

"Not too good," he said. "Look, I've got some money saved up and nothing much to do with it. Any chance you'd be interested in going to school with the Catholics? It's small. A close friend of mine runs the place."

"Really? Who's your close friend, God?"

Mr. Fielding laughed. "Father Tim. He's a good guy. We've known each other a while. I'm what you might call a backsliding Catholic, but him I like. He sort of...well, I guess he understands me better than most. And he knows how to run a school. I told him about you."

"A private school sounds like a lot of work."

"Try it for a week, and I'll let you drive the car."

And that's how I ended up at Holy Cross. I was only fourteen, but Mr. Fielding pulled off at the next I-5 exit and we switched places. We took back roads all the way to Gravy's and I drove the whole way. Three weeks later I stepped foot into Holy Cross.

If I trace the whole thing back, it was the food and the driving that led to the disaster. If it weren't for the long lazy drives in search of each other and a crispy plate of hash browns, we never would have hit the tree.

TWELVE DAYS TO MIDNIGHT

3:00 PM
TUESDAY, OCTOBER 9TH

"*Come on, Fielding*. It's like twenty minutes, is all. What's your problem?"

This was classic Ethan. He had me cornered while I waited in the parking lot for Oh and Milo to show up.

"I told you already, I have plans. I didn't even bring my racquet."

"Don't give me that crap. Walk three steps and you'll trip over ten racquets in this place. Come on, man! The courts are filling up."

"You don't have any balls," I said.

"Har har har. Never heard that one before."

"Your balls are all wet."

"Keep it coming, smart guy. If you're too chicken to play me just say so."

"I'm too chicken to play you. And your balls are yellow."

Ethan let out a screech of laughter, and this time it had an angry edge to it.

Besides the howler, one of the most annoying things about Ethan is apparently he's very good-looking. You know how when you see a girl and she's thirteen, but if you see her from behind you'd swear she was twenty-one? I'd say something like that is true of Ethan. Sideburns, muscles, broad shoulders, not a zit on him. From the back I'd take him for twenty-five, easy. Plus he's rich. He has a brand-new two-tone MINI Cooper for which he contributed not one penny and got the second he turned sixteen.

Good looks, decent athlete, tons of dough, hot car. It takes a lot of strikes to turn a guy with all that going for him into a pariah. If you add it all up, Ethan has two basic problems: very obnoxious, and full of himself. But around Holy Cross, that's not nearly enough to knock him off the Prom King platform given all the pluses stacked in his favor.

"You know what this is like?" he went on. Once Ethan made up his mind he was like a pit bull clamped onto a turkey bone. "It's like leaving a poker table with everyone's money before they're ready to give up. It's a wuss move, Fielding."

The last time I played Ethan, nobody at our school had beaten him all year. I don't even like tennis that much, and I beat him four games to three. When it was over, he threw his one-hundred-twenty-dollar Prince in my general direction.

"Yo, Ethan! We need a fourth. Come on," yelled Nick. He was standing on one of Holy Cross's two courts with Phil. Marissa Barstow (hot, popular, decent backhand) was standing on the other side all alone. Ethan and Marissa were on again, off again. They were currently off again.

He pointed a finger in my face and started backpedaling. "Tomorrow—I'm serious. Don't wimp out on me, Fielding. Rain or shine, you're going down."

Oh and Milo had finally emerged from inside the school. Milo's plume of black hair and combat boots gave him a perceived height advantage over Oh of about an eighth of an inch. If you shaved his head and put him in bare feet he'd be a good two inches shorter than she was. Milo is a very interesting guy, but I had the height advantage with Oh.

"Is he always like that?" asked Oh.

"Ethan is just pissed Jacob beat him," said Milo. "I hope Phil doesn't take one in the face. YO KICK HIS ASS, PHIL!"

Phil gave us the thumbs-up as one of Marissa's wailer backhands sailed over the net, missing him by about a foot.

"The rain's stopped and I'm dying to ride," said Oh. "Let's get some food."

Oh took her longboard out of the back of Milo's car, and in the span of about sixty seconds transformed into something I liked even more. She unbuttoned the top of her olive green school uniform, revealing a Jack Skellington T-shirt underneath. Then she tied her hair back in a ponytail and pulled her red cap over her head.

I got in the car and rolled the window down.

"*Nightmare Before Christmas,*" I said from the passenger seat of Milo's car, referring to her T-shirt. "Milo give you that?"

"Nope. Found it at that thrift shop downtown where me and Milo met. Can you believe people just give this stuff away?"

Milo pulled out and started driving at about five miles per hour while Oh held on to the door through the open window on my side and rolled along on her longboard. Her fingers peeked out from under the pink cast and I noticed she still hadn't let anyone else sign it.

"Speed bump," warned Milo.

"I'm not blind," said Oh. "Take it up a notch, Grandpa."

Oh took the speed bump like it was butter, looking out over the empty soccer field in front of the school.

"I love soccer," she said. "I miss it."

"Speed bump," said Milo. He was going about ten, the legal limit on the school driveway.

Oh leaned down into the window and I caught the smell of her hair in the wind.

"Milo, I swear to God, if you don't shut up..." The speed bump came under the board and Oh's head hit the rim of the door pretty hard.

"Sorry about that, but you can't say I didn't warn you," said Milo.

"You okay?" I asked.

"Didn't hurt a bit."

38

"You should wear a helmet."

"Speed bump."

Oh laughed, like a song that starts soft and ends in a whisper. Her hips moved up, then down as she crested the bump. I wanted to touch her fingers, the ones sticking out of the pink cast. I wanted to hold her hand.

Milo slowed as we approached the end of the drive. It sloped down and ended on Haysville Boulevard, a winding two-way road that was marginally busy this time of day. From the window of my science classroom, the cars on Haysville looked as if they were moving in slow motion, like they couldn't hurt a fly.

"See you later, boys," said Oh.

She had let herself roll back, closer to the side door, stretching her arms along the length of the back window. When Milo applied the brakes, she pulled herself forward and flew past like she'd been released from a slingshot. She smiled, invigorated.

"You're crazy!" I shouted.

Everything was slow-mo. I could feel the cool, damp air in my eyes. I could smell the muddy soccer field. Oh was gliding, like on a surfboard, a beautiful girl riding a concrete wave toward a sidewalk beach.

Oh soared past the hood of Milo's car. She'd had it in her head to veer in front of the car, keep going left, and catch the sidewalk along the road. She could have been perfectly fine, because she really had nailed the timing and the distance, fast and in control.

But a rock the size of a marble is the mortal enemy of a skateboarder. It's why boarders hate skateparks that are shared by BMXers. Rubber wheels pick up rocks and carry them onto the glassy smooth surface, and that equals a face-plant if you're riding and the pebble finds your wheel. I know, I've done it.

Oh pitched forward and sideways at once with distressing speed and threw her cast-covered arm out in front of herself. It was too much force for a broken limb, and her elbow buckled under her own weight. I heard her face hit the pavement, a loud crack, like a baseball bat against a telephone pole.

Then she slid on her hands. Her palms had to be shredding as she slid out past the sidewalk and into the road. These events seemed to take place in a vacuum, a timeless moment that could have been an hour or a split second.

I had my foot on the pavement seconds after Oh hit the rock. I yelled her name. It sounded peculiar, shouting *Oh* like that, an exclamation of surprise.

I arrived at Oh's body first, Milo right behind me. She was badly injured, had to be, and I yelled at Milo to go back and slam on his car horn and yell for help.

Oh sat up slowly and looked at her hands, then turned and looked at me, awe in her hazel eyes.

I knelt down in front of her, shocked she wasn't wailing or knocked out. She touched her own face and head carefully while we listened to Milo hit his horn over and over and yell for help. She clenched her hand into a fist and back out again.

"What just happened to me?" she asked.

Cars on the road next to the sidewalk slowed and rolled their windows down, asking if Oh was all right.

Of course she's not all right! I thought. *She smashed her face into the pavement!*

But I couldn't bring myself to say the words, because what I was seeing didn't add up. No blood. No anything.

"What just happened to me?" Oh asked again.

"Don't move," I said. "Just stay still." I reached out and touched her on the back and had an instant and totally inappropriate desire to kiss her. Tears were streaming down my face but I was laughing.

"This has to be a dream," I said, touching her face and her hands. "This can't be right."

Oh smiled as Milo came alongside of us with a perplexed look on his face.

"It's okay," she said. "I'm fine...I think."

Despite my protests, she stood up and wiped the dirt off her shirt.

"There's not a scratch on you," said Milo. And there wasn't. Her pants had a rip in them at the knee and her shirt was wet and dirty, but there wasn't a single thing wrong with Ophelia James. No broken nose, no shattered teeth, no missing skin on her palms, nothing. She was perfect.

The foursome who'd been playing tennis on the courts in

front of the school ran toward us on the soccer field, Ethan out in front.

"Where'd my hat go?" asked Oh. Her cap had flown off her head and landed in the road where it was being run over by a passing pickup truck. I darted out into the road to retrieve it.

By the time Ethan and the rest arrived, breathless and expecting a scene, Oh had her hat back on and was looking as flawlessly beautiful as ever.

I remember feeling protective of Oh when she picked up her longboard and examined it for damage. I kept thinking we were dealing with some sort of post-traumatic event and any second she would drop dead in a pile of broken bones.

I once heard a story like that about a car accident. A mom and two little kids were racing through an intersection and got sideswiped by an SUV. This lady undid her seat belt, climbed into the backseat, and took hold of her two little kids. Then she opened the passenger door, got out, and set them down. About five seconds later she collapsed with a broken neck and a concussion. She never walked again after that.

"Ophelia James," said Ethan, looking at her disheveled hair and torn pants. "What a piece of work."

"Shut up, Anderson," said Marissa, more than a little jealous.

"Don't have a cow. I'm only stating the obvious—"

That did it. Marissa went after him with her racquet,

and Ethan and Nick and Phil all laughed until she stalked back to the courts without them.

"Come on, M, don't be so sensitive," Ethan said.

Marissa yelled over her shoulder, "Don't call me that!"

"The rain's gonna start up again," said Nick. He lined up a slow-motion backhand as he talked. "Just go make up with her and let's play."

The three of them wandered off, laughing and chatting as if there'd been no accident to begin with. The whole event seemed blurry to me already, like memories of my mom.

"You never answered my question," said Oh, turning back to me.

"What question?" asked Milo.

She looked at me like I knew something I wasn't telling her.

"What just *happened* to me?"

I stood there, confused and tongue-tied. Something wasn't right, I could feel it. I still half expected Oh to drop dead.

"I've gotta go," I said.

And then I ran like I've always run when the smell of danger gets too close.

◆　◆　◆

8:00 PM: *Where did you go?*

The text message came from a number I didn't recognize. Oh. Milo had already called and texted a half-dozen times and I hadn't replied.

I sat on my bed in a kind of trance with Mr. Fielding's Zippo, lighting it, running my fingers over the flames, slapping the metal lid shut. I had information they didn't know about, facts that were important, but I wasn't ready to face them quite yet. But in the last text, Milo had said they were coming over whether I liked it or not.

7:00 PM: *We're picking you up @ 8.15. parking lot. don't be late*

7:12 PM: *Going to loft*

7:16 PM: *Bring homework. hahaha*

7:21 PM: *Don't go dark on me again*

7:48 PM: *It's raining. bring a hat*

8:06 PM: *Be there in 15. you better be walking*

The phone rang in my hand. Father Tim from Seattle.

"You playing with that lighter again?" asked Father Tim. Dang. I snapped it shut. He coveted the lighter, I knew, and probably wondered if I was doing it harm.

"Don't worry, I'm not going to burn the place down."

"That's a relief. How are the old guys doing? Are they feeding you?"

"They're trying. How can you eat Frank's cooking? Scary."

"The smoking helps. Kills the taste buds. Top shelf in my office has Pop-Tarts if you get desperate."

I started down the hall, cell phone in one hand, lighter in the other.

"How'd it go at Holy Cross today?"

Turning into Father Tim's office I caught the damp odor of spent cigarettes and old newspapers.

44

"Smells like a hobo has set up shop in your study," I said.

"Took a long time to get it that way. Don't clean up."

I fished a pack of cherry Pop-Tarts out of a crumpled box on Father Tim's shelf and returned to my room.

"So, how'd it go?" he persisted. Did he really want dad duty now that Mr. Fielding was gone?

"It was fine, boring, nothing happened." I heard the poorly concealed irritation in my own voice.

"You know," he said, pausing to take a drag on his cigarette. I could imagine the smoke drifting out of his nose as he spoke, see him flicking ashes off his black polyester pants. "It's okay to miss him. I miss him. I knew him about as well as anyone."

"I doubt that," I said, jealous at the thought of all the time Father Tim had enjoyed with Mr. Fielding. It also made me wonder just how much Father Tim knew. And what he'd tell.

Another long pause.

"He talked about you," he said finally. "A lot."

"I gotta go," I said, sitting up and glancing at my watch, realizing I was going to be late meeting Milo and Oh.

"You're sure everything's okay?" he asked again.

"Yeah, honestly—school was fine. Same as it always is. Get back soon so we can figure things out."

I pulled the phone from my ear, and heard him say, "Be careful with that lighter," as I hung up.

I didn't feel like packing up my stuff and running from

Oh and Milo. The three of us had been involved in something we all knew didn't make sense, and the only way I was going to sort this out was by talking to them, telling them the truth about what had happened. Or at least part of the truth.

There's a shortcut through the woods between the church house and the school that is generally avoided by students. It's not officially off-limits, but there's a grim urban legend about the shortcut involving a student, two severed fingers, and an escapee from the state mental hospital. The hospital isn't that far from the school and the story is pretty good, so it tends to keep the woods empty of people. Still, it's twice as long to use the neighborhood roads, so I started up the soggy path and felt the wet branches wipe against my jacket.

8:12 PM: We're here...where are you?

I passed by a rotting tree trunk and smelled the air thicken, tapping out a message that said: *Be there in 3 min, minus 2 fingers.*

Thick, tangled walls of blackberry enclosed the narrow path as I wound my way closer to the school. The rolling hills of snarled thorn had ruled the woods for decades, wrapping around moss-covered trees and rising a dozen feet in the air through gray fog.

The parking lot was empty when I cleared the woods, and I knew that Milo hadn't actually arrived yet. He didn't have the patience to wait for people. I texted one word: *liar.*

My feet wanted to run as I watched the headlights turn onto the long drive and my phone buzzed.

8:16 PM: *shut your pie hole*

I laughed out loud as the car pulled up and I got into the backseat, feeling better than I'd expected to.

"You shouldn't use your phone while you're driving. It's dangerous," I said.

"Hi," said Oh from the front seat, but she didn't turn toward me. It was the first time since I'd met her that I couldn't read her face and make a guess at what she was thinking. Something along the lines of *Milo and I have been talking about you. We're not sure what to think. What's wrong with you?*

I didn't like the way it felt, being on the outside. I'd only known Oh for a day. It shouldn't have bothered me that she might feel more at ease with my best friend than she did with me. But it did.

"Look, you guys, I'm sorry I flipped out."

"It's cool," said Milo. He swung the car around and started through the low fog, glancing at the passenger seat. "Things are cool, right, Oh?"

She spun around so she could see me in the dim light. "I've never seen anyone run away from me like that before."

I couldn't think of what to say so I just sat there, stupid-faced, staring back at her. We turned onto Haysville Boulevard, and I remembered the sound of Oh's forehead hitting the sidewalk.

"I've got something to tell you guys," I said, coughing

a frog out of my throat. "But I'd rather say it at the loft if that's okay."

Oh looked between me and Milo, eyes narrowed, making a cute crinkle in the center of her forehead, and I couldn't help thinking there should have been a huge gash and a jagged line of fifty stitches in place of her perfectly smooth skin.

"I've never done a face-plant like that before without breaking something or drawing blood," she said. "Actually, I've never fallen that hard in my life." There was a glint of fear in her voice that I hadn't heard before.

"It would have made a stellar YouTube video," said Milo. He was doing a seat-of-his-pants dance in the driver's seat. "The title could have been a killer: 'Hot clumsy girl eats concrete.'"

Oh laughed softly, but it was a disturbing image and I couldn't get it out of my head. *Hot clumsy girl eats concrete.* It didn't feel like we'd safely arrived at a moment where we could start joking about Oh miraculously escaping injury.

The loft wasn't too far off, only about a mile and the roads were clear, and I focused on the simple things as we made our way. *Keep it light, small talk, lots of open spaces, pretend like you're texting someone.*

Up Lancaster, right on Market, into the old downtown, park the car, and walk up to the black door.

"*This* is the loft?" asked Oh, reading the sign over the door. "*Coffin Books.* Don't your parents own this place?"

Milo nodded and inserted a key, turning the dead bolt. He held the door open and I went inside, followed by Oh.

"This place smells like dead books," she observed. "Like old stuff no one reads."

"You'd be surprised," I said, staring into the darkness.

"My parents let us use it to study after hours as long as we don't move anything or monkey with the register."

"We like to monkey with the register," I said. "It's been a problem."

"Okaaaay…" said Oh. "Is there a light in this place or do you write term papers in the dark?"

I'd been inside Coffin Books so many times before, it was no problem zigzagging in the shadows until I reached the far wall and flicked on the overhead lights.

"Can I give you the nickel tour?" Milo asked.

Watching Milo maneuver Oh around the room made me think he should quit school, move to Chicago, and shuttle families around the Field Museum.

"Two book lovers on the tail end of financial doom are what got this place started ten years ago. My parents worked in tech, made and lost a ton of dough, and ended up with a basement full of books. When they had money to spend, this is what they spent it on."

Oh scanned the shelves filled with thousands of old volumes, mouthing some of the titles.

"The books in here are all a little on the dark side. Strange fantasy, classic horror, end of times science fiction, hard-to-find mystery novels—a lot of stuff that's out of print. That's what they're into, don't ask me why."

Mr. Fielding and I were both into sci-fi books, and there

was no place better than Coffin Books to get them. But once I'd met Milo, he and I would end up hanging out in the loft while Mr. Fielding and Mr. Coffin wandered down a dusty aisle of books.

Milo pointed to each of the seven floor-to-ceiling rows like a flight attendant indicating the exits, which got me and Oh laughing and stealing glances at one another. Her look was a combination of *Is he serious?* and *I love this place.*

Coffin Books had a medieval charm in the few places where books weren't gobbling up all the space. One such item, a set of armor, stood behind the service counter.

"My dad collects junk like that," said Milo. "You should see the basement."

There were iron shackles, chain mail, swords, and other paraphernalia high out of reach above the shelves. It was all very Vincent Price, spooky kind of stuff you'd expect to see in an old movie with a dungeon and lots of torture devices.

"That's the loft." Milo pointed. "You can only reach it from a sliding ladder on wheels. If someone moves the ladder while you're in the loft, well, that's your problem."

"This is the place?" asked Oh. She walked confidently to the sliding ladder, rolled it under the loft, and looked back at us. "What are we waiting for?"

♦ ♦ ♦

There were four cushy chairs in the loft and a good-sized round table in the middle where a guy could put his feet up.

The table was strewn with books and a day-old newspaper someone had left behind. The light was soft and yellow. A black iron rail with metal crows welded through the middle surrounded the loft. It was a good place to read, a place where an entire day could disappear.

"I think I know why Oh didn't get hurt when she fell," I began hesitantly. We each sat in a chair facing one another as the grandfather clock downstairs signaled 9:00 PM. Oh had the bottoms of her skate shoes against the edge of the table, as if it were a skateboard she wanted to ride.

"Maybe it's just a fluke, the way she went down," said Milo. "Stranger things have happened."

"No, that's not right," said Oh. "I've only fallen hard three times. I'm not a street skater. You don't get a longboard to do tricks—it's *transportation*, you guys. The first time I fell was the day I got it. I was coming out of our garage and hit a concrete seam in the driveway. The board stopped and I kept going. My palms were a bloody mess, and both my knees turned blue and swelled up. It hurt. I mean, it *really* hurt. I didn't even ride for a week."

"And the second time you broke your wrist?" I asked.

Oh held up her arm, shaking the cast back and forth slowly.

"The funny thing is I didn't even fall that hard. Maybe my wrist was weak from falling the first time. I don't know. It just snapped."

"The third fall was today, then," said Milo. He touched

the weak black fuzz on his chin and stared at the round table. "And it didn't hurt at all, not even under the cast?"

"Obviously I'm not being totally clear about this," said Oh. "Either that or you're just not listening. I didn't feel *any* pain."

"That is a little odd, I guess," Milo said.

Oh stared at me, her eyes even more brilliantly hazel in the yellow light.

I could have run away, forgotten the accident had ever happened, and moved on with my boring life at the church house. But for some stupid reason I couldn't stay quiet anymore. I was probably trying to impress Oh or Milo or both.

It was a terrible decision I came to regret.

"Do you know how Mr. Fielding died?" I asked Oh, but Milo answered.

"Dude, everyone knows that much."

So she knew about the slippery road, knew we'd slammed into the wide trunk of an ancient tree.

"When we swerved off the road," I began, hesitating. "He said something to me."

"What was it? What did Mr. Fielding say to you?" asked Oh. Her feet were back on the floor and she was leaning almost all the way over the table.

"The same thing I wrote on your cast."

Oh lolled her head sideways and looked at me funny, like she was processing a long math problem.

"Here I thought you were a poet," said Oh. "I'm so disappointed."

"Hey, it's still the best note anyone's ever written on a cast," Milo reassured me.

"You guys don't get it," I said.

I reached into my pocket and pulled out Mr. Fielding's Zippo. It was a lighter with a story all its own, but for now the only important thing was that it worked.

I flicked the Zippo open and spun the dial, catching a whiff of lighter fluid as the flame shot up. Then I put my palm directly over the flame and let it burn.

"Stop that!" cried Oh. "You're crazy!"

She reached over the table and tried to knock the lighter out of my hand, but I was too quick.

"What's your problem?" asked Milo.

Ten seconds, fifteen, and the flame stayed nice and fat against the skin of my palm.

"Jacob, *please*!" said Oh. She began to sound as though she might cry. I pulled the flame away and held up my hand.

"You guys, I'm fine. I didn't feel a thing," I said, looking into Oh's eyes as she began to calm down. "Just like you on your longboard."

She shook her head, more angry than excited by what I was saying. "What the hell is going on, Jacob?"

Her eyes stole across my face and to the ladder leading down to the door where she could escape. I understood the urge well. I tried to imagine what she was thinking, what meeting me had led to in a few short hours.

"I made a mistake," I said. "But it probably saved your life."

"This is messed up," said Milo. "It makes no sense."

"What are you saying?" asked Oh.

In the five hours between the time I'd run away and when Milo and Oh had showed up in the school parking lot, I'd had a chance to really think things through.

"This isn't something I can tell you," I said. "I have to show you."

Oh wiped a tear that hadn't found its way completely out of her eye.

"Show us, wonder boy."

◆　◆　◆

"We were driving along," I began, my voice quiet in the soft light of the loft. "Me and Mr. Fielding, and it happened without warning. We were doing sixty when we hit the tree. Have you ever stood up close to an old growth on the way to the coast? The trunks are ten feet around at the bottom. Hitting one with a car is no different than slamming into a wall of granite. I shouldn't have survived, let alone come away uninjured."

"Right...," Oh said very slowly, as if trying to process everything one bit at a time.

"Mr. Fielding *transferred* something to me when he said those words, and then I transferred it to Oh. It's the only explanation."

"You've lost your mind," said Milo.

"I would agree if it weren't for all the evidence piling up.

How else do we explain it? We hit a giant tree doing sixty. *Sixty*, Milo. I should be dead right along with Mr. Fielding, but I walked away without a scratch. I can hold a flame against my skin for as long as I want. Oh face-planted onto the pavement today and didn't feel a thing. I'm not crazy."

"Give me the lighter," said Oh, holding out her hand above the round table filled with books. I watched the excitement flash across her face.

"I don't think that's a good idea."

"Then give it to me," said Milo. "I want in on this. Say those words to me and let's see if it works."

I waited, not sure what to do, glancing back and forth between the two of them.

Oh piped in: "Come on, Jacob, just say it to one of us. Don't you want to see if it actually works like you think it does?"

I couldn't tell if Oh was serious or joking. Either she didn't trust me or she really was curious.

"I held the flame under my hand for ten minutes at the church house," I said. "Trust me, it works."

"Then it must still work for me, too," said Oh. She lifted her pink cast over the table, intent on slamming it down hard enough to jar the broken bone inside.

"Oh—don't!" I yelled. "I took it back!"

She held her arm over the table, letting it hover there long enough to really think it through.

"What do you mean you took it back?"

"I mean you don't have it anymore."

"How do you know we don't both have it? And how did you take it back?" she asked.

"It was an accident, just like when I gave it to you."

This came out all wrong, like I'd never meant to save Oh in the first place, so I started again.

"What I mean is, I was lying on my bed, staring at the ceiling, thinking about when we met and what all happened. I got to the part where I wrote those words on your cast."

"You mean these words?" asked Oh, rolling over her cast and pointing the words in my face.

"Yeah, I mean those. I kept saying them, whispering them, but something didn't feel right. It was like something outside was trying to get back in, but couldn't unless I did something different. So I said it another way. *I am indestructible.* And I could...I don't know...I could *feel* it come back into me."

"That's freaky," said Milo.

"And after that," I went on, staring at Oh, "I had this feeling that you weren't safe anymore but that I was. Like nothing could harm me. That's when I took out the lighter."

The pink cast swayed over the table for another moment, then Oh gave up the idea and leaned heavily in her chair.

"Say it to Milo," said Oh. "I'll hit him and then you can take it back. That's how we'll test it."

"This whole thing is a joke," said Milo. "It *can't* be real."

I wanted to agree with Milo and hoped he was right, but

we weren't going to get to the bottom of things unless the three of us could agree on what *it* was.

"You are indestructible."

Milo took in a deep, exaggerated breath. "I feel like I could jump off the Empire State Building."

"Don't joke around," said Oh. "This is serious."

"Come on," said Milo. He glanced from me to Oh, half smiling and half nervous that one of us was about to punch him in the face.

"Put your hand on the table," Oh commanded.

Milo shook his head in disbelief. "For God's sake, be careful," he said, slowly reaching his hand out and fanning his fingers against the wood. "I have a chemistry test tomorrow. I'm going to need those fingers."

Oh lifted her pink cast and slammed Milo across the knuckles with a solid blow. She cried out, cradling her broken arm like a baby as she pulled her knees up to her chest and fell back into the chair.

I had been tricked. She had wanted to test herself and Milo at once, and she'd managed to do it. We all knew instantly that Oh did not have any unexplainable power of protection.

"I knew this was a bad idea," I shouted, bolting around the table next to her.

She hid her face behind her hair. "I hit it a lot harder than that on the sidewalk," she responded in a cracked voice.

"Hey, you guys…," said Milo.

Oh pushed her hair back and we both looked at Milo

together. He was making a fist and stretching his fingers out over and over.

"Didn't feel a thing." He laughed and shook his head. "Craziest thing I ever saw."

Oh picked up a book from the table with her good hand.

"Hold still."

The smile evaporated from Milo's face as Oh reeled back and threw the book. It was big, it was a hardback, and it tagged Milo right in the nose.

"That's for making my arm hurt," said Oh.

"Doesn't bother me a bit! In fact I sort of enjoyed it! Keep it coming."

Milo was really getting into the idea, and I have to admit it was entertaining to watch. I was smiling, too—at least until Oh turned her violent intentions on me. Without the slightest warning she leaned forward and punched me in the shoulder. Don't let anyone tell you a girl can't hit hard when she wants to.

"You felt that?" asked Oh inquisitively. She was about as curious as I'd seen her all day. Something about the experimenting really turned her wheels.

"Yes, I felt it," I answered, rubbing the sting out of my arm.

Oh was looking at me like I was a lab rat she'd just spun around her head by the tail and I was standing drunkenly on an examination table.

"I barely hit you," said Oh. "It was a love tap."

"I'd hate to see you when you're angry."

Milo had his thumb on the table and kept hitting it with the book Oh had thrown at him. He looked like a lunatic, raising the book as high as he could and cracking the spine against his own thumb.

I was starting to feel more curious myself and couldn't help advancing our experimentation by closing my eyes and saying the words to myself.

I am indestructible.

About three seconds later Milo hit himself again, and this time he felt it. He threw the book out of the loft as if it were a football. The pages fluttered until the spine hit a shelf and the book spun wildly.

"Good idea, take it out on the book," I muttered.

Milo kept shaking his hand and cussing up a storm, but Oh didn't say another word. She seemed to be drinking everything in, calculating the different possibilities.

"You said it, didn't you?" she asked. Oh wasn't staring at me, but I knew it was me she was asking.

"Thanks a lot, bro," said Milo. "Next time a little warning might be nice."

"I didn't say anything," I replied, thinking about what I *had* done.

"*God* this is confusing," said Oh.

"I didn't say it out loud, but I thought it."

"Interesting," said Oh. "So you thought the words and now Milo's thumb is broken."

"It's not broken, not even close. It's fine."

The loft isn't that big to begin with, but Oh was closer than I expected. She looked up, and then she touched the side of my face with the fingers from her broken arm, sending my pulse into overdrive.

"I think he'll be okay," she said, and smiled beautifully.

I was a bit too mesmerized by Oh to see Milo pick up the book. He threw it at my gut like a Frisbee. It hit a little low, right where it counts, and I buckled over.

"Why'd you throw it so hard?" yelled Oh.

"I didn't throw it that hard, just lower than I planned. Sorry, dude," Milo said, laughing and wincing at once. It sounded like this was Oh's idea, and she'd probably given Milo a wink and a nod while I wasn't looking.

I stood up straight and realized that the blow actually hadn't hurt a bit. Such a strange feeling: expecting yourself to be hurt and finding you're not.

I could imagine how experiencing the world like this, a world where you couldn't be damaged, could become addicting.

"I have to be home by ten thirty or I'm in big trouble," Oh said, interrupting our little torture-fest.

"You're kidding me," said Milo.

"You don't know my mom. She'll seriously ground me. We're not going to make any progress figuring this out if I'm locked up at home after school."

"Well, this has been fun," I said. "Let's do it again real soon." I got courtesy laughs all around as Milo started down the ladder.

"Wait here a second," Oh said. "We have time for one more test if we make it fast."

I waited at the top of the ladder as she raced down two rungs at a time. When she reached the bottom, she pushed the ladder on its wheels and it rolled away.

"Um...a little help here," I said.

"Jump," said Oh.

From the loft to the floor in Coffin Books was maybe twelve or thirteen feet. Not the biggest jump ever, but high enough in the dim yellow light with all sorts of unsteady stuff to land on. Piles of books, tables, chairs—there wasn't a clear space more than two feet square anywhere I looked.

"Come on, Jacob, I gotta go," said Oh, looking at her watch. "It's twenty after. If I'm late, it's your fault."

"Push the ladder back over," I said.

Oh just stared at me, smiling. There was nowhere to run. "You're indestructible, remember? This should be a walk in the park."

"Just do it, man," said Milo. "Worst-case scenario you'll twist an ankle. Come on! We gotta go!"

I took a couple of deep breaths, set my sights on a patch of open space next to a lamp and a chair, and went for it.

There are at least two bummers about falling on a floor lamp. One, they can be sharp, a little bit like a spear with a shade on top. The lamp I fell toward was of the standing, gothic variety, with a thin post made of metal.

The second bummer about falling on a lamp is they can

be loaded with electricity. If a lamp is turned on and you've jumped in its general direction, then your IQ is probably on par with a block of cheese.

I hit the top of the lamp with the inside of my arm, where the lightbulb exploded into sparks and glass. The sharpest part of the bottom of the bulb punctured right through my light jacket and touched my skin. The lamp tipped over and the broken glass ripped a long cut into the arm of my jacket. My head hit a thin old rug that lay over the hardwood floor, and I rolled into a neck-bending somersault.

"Don't touch him!" Oh cried out.

"It's okay," I said. "I think I'm fine."

But I could see by the way they were looking at me that something wasn't right. I looked to my right and saw little sparks popping under my arm—and going into my body.

"If you touch him he'll conduct," Oh said to Milo. "You'll be just as fried as he should be."

I grabbed the middle of the lamp and pulled it free from my jacket. There was a popping sound and the whole room went dark. A dusty beam of weak light showed itself from the street as I stood up and started checking myself for damage.

"I'm fine, you guys," I said. This time, I heard the wonder in my own voice and realized for the first time how dangerous the situation had become. I felt the surprising touch of Oh's hand on mine in the dark. It was trembling but warm.

Milo stumbled around looking for a flashlight or a candle, mumbling a string of thoughts out loud. "This is crazy... makes no sense... my dad's gonna be pissed... damn it!"

"I'm sorry," Oh whispered, shockingly close to my ear.

"What's wrong?" I asked, because she sounded different, like she was the one who had been hurt in my fall. She pulled away and spoke out loud.

"Nothing. It's just... I don't know, I don't feel so good. I think I'm going to be sick."

"Hold on! Not in the store!" yelled Milo. He'd found a flashlight behind the counter and turned it on. "I've got enough explaining to do already!"

Milo guided Oh outside and she threw up in the gutter, leaning heavily against the car on her bad wrist. We made small talk and tried to pretend like we weren't paying any attention. What girl wants to be seen puking her guts out in front of two guys?

Oh stood up and wiped her arm across her lips, turning to us.

"Got any towels?"

"Yeah, I mean, no," I said. I peeled off my ripped jacket and draped it over her shoulders. I was wearing a T-shirt and she touched my arm on the inside near my elbow, where the skin is soft and vulnerable. Her fingers moved, searching for a gash or a wide cut, but there was nothing to find.

Oh wiped her face with one of the dangling sleeves of

my coat. "I think I'm okay now. Can you guys just take me home?"

We got in the car and no one said anything for a long time. We just watched the lights change, listened to the tires on wet pavement. She lived in one of the older, run-down apartment buildings on the edge of town. I don't know why I expected any different, but—maybe because she seemed so perfect to me—I was a little bit surprised to discover she was living in a less-than-ideal setting.

"Ten twenty-nine," said Milo. "Back to the castle with a minute to spare."

"You want me to walk you up?" I asked from the back-seat.

She didn't answer my question, just shook her head as I jumped out and stood next to her.

"See you tomorrow?" I asked. I had a sinking feeling our weird night together had changed things, maybe not for the better.

"Yeah. Can I keep your coat?"

"Of course, yeah, keep it. Maybe sew it up if you get a chance."

Oh smiled up at me and walked away, and I got in the front seat with Milo.

"Why do I feel like a third wheel all of a sudden?" said Milo, pulling around the parking lot and scrolling through his iPod with one hand.

"Couldn't tell you. How's that thumb doing?"

"Hurts to find music, but I'll live."

We drove in awkward silence.

We'd started something none of us understood, and it was impossible to know where it would lead.

ELEVEN DAYS TO MIDNIGHT

WEDNESDAY, OCTOBER 10TH

It felt like a month between the first and last class of the day, stealing moments between bells to pass ideas back and forth as secretly as we could. What little we whispered back and forth in the halls consisted almost entirely of useless snippets.

I've got an idea, something we should try.

No texting about this, just in case someone sees and takes one of our phones.

That would be a disaster.

Meet in the parking lot after school.

You still have it pointed on yourself, right?

That last one came from Oh, who snuck up behind me with a sharp pencil pointed into my back. When I nodded, she pushed, softly at first, then quite a bit harder.

"Still working?"

"Nope. You've just given me lead poisoning. I think you pierced my heart."

"They don't actually use lead in these things anymore. It's graphite."

When she turned in the direction of her next class, her hand slid across my back and she glanced back, smiling. I started to think it was probably time to have a talk with Milo about how she wouldn't come between us, because I was already planning out exactly where I was taking her for our first official date. Now all I had to do was get up enough courage to ask her.

Holy Cross was too small for team sports to catch on big, because no one knew from one year to the next if we'd have enough good players to field a competitive team. Individual sports ruled and Father Tim loved tennis. It was like a blood sport at Holy Cross. Throughout the day, Ethan bugged me endlessly to get my ass on the court and give up the crown. He wouldn't leave me alone at lunch, and I finally had to give in. Either I played or we'd be putting up with his harassing us every second.

"Kick his ass and do it fast," Milo grumbled as we parted ways before the last class of the day. "We've got more important things to deal with."

"Just let him win," suggested Oh. She and I headed toward religion class, taught by Father Tim. We were all surprised to see he'd returned a day early from Seattle.

"You were expecting an easy go of it with Father Blake," he began, pacing back and forth in front of his desk. "No such luck today."

Father Blake was a retired priest from the church house who treated his occasional class sessions as study halls. He couldn't hear very well and he cleared his throat into a handkerchief about ten times every hour.

Father Tim, having had lots of time on the drive to and from Seattle to think, kicked off the class with a loaded question, which was how many of his classes began.

"Who in this classroom is going to hell?"

A few kids laughed, three hands shot up, and Ethan pointed at me.

Despite Ethan's finger in my face, Father Tim's question had inadvertently made me wonder about my own mortality.

If I was indestructible, could I also live forever?

I didn't know, but the idea of it was startling.

The question itself was no doubt some kind of trick, had to be. Despite Father Tim's standard priest garb of black button-down and white collar, the clothing, in my opinion, did not match the man. His theology was like a gray fog: nothing black and white about it. He never wanted an automatic catechism answer from his students. He wanted us to really *ponder* his questions.

Who in this classroom is going to hell?

Oh looked at me, I looked at her. We smiled. It was very distracting.

"Is Mr. Bo Jangles going to hell?" asked Father Tim.

This got a laugh out of almost everyone along with a lot of head nodding, because Mr. Bo Jangles was a huge orange library cat with a reputation campus-wide as a hand-scratching cuff-biter.

"That cat is doomed," said Ethan.

Father Tim, pulling us deeper into the mire of the problem, wasted no time responding.

"Why would you say that? What motivation would God have for sending a cat to hell?"

"Come on, Father, Bo is a monster. He hates kids."

"Humans hate," said Father Tim. "Animals do what they are designed to do, and the design does not include emotions."

He pointed to Oh, who had raised her hand unexpectedly.

"I disagree. Our dog has emotions."

Father Tim smiled politely.

"Scientific evidence suggests otherwise. You only think your dog is happy or sad or mean, but he isn't really."

"It's a she, and yes, she does."

"What's the dog's name?"

"Clarisse."

"All right then, let's talk about Clarisse. You pet Clarisse and she wags her tail and you think—ah! Look at that! My dog is happy. But what if she is only reacting out of instinct in a way that makes you *think* she's happy?"

"What does this have to do with hell?" asked Ethan.

Oh pressed on. "If instincts and emotions have the same result, then what's the difference between them? I come home and Clarisse is excited to see me. She's happy."

"Do you think Clarisse could be angry with you? Would she want to hurt your feelings if you withhold the food bowl?"

"There's not a mean bone in her body. Mr. Bo Jangles got them all."

I was starting to see Father Tim's point. I raised my hand and he pointed to me.

"An animal doesn't kill because it's mad; it kills because that's how it's designed. So like a lion kills an antelope. It's not angry, it's just hungry, and for a lion that's okay. Humans kill each other for totally different reasons."

"And lions don't have a conscience," said Ethan.

Father Tim stepped to the blackboard and wrote the word *conscience* in white chalk. As the word appeared, I thought about how they probably didn't have old-school chalkboards at South Ridge.

"Does Clarisse have a conscience?"

He pointed to the word, looked back at Oh.

"Maybe."

"What if she and Mr. Bo Jangles were to have it out, claws and all, and the cat was killed. Would Clarisse care?"

"Maybe."

"Your maybes aren't very useful, I'm afraid, but I see your difficulty. You want Clarisse to feel things she cannot feel."

"I disagree. Clarisse feels some things, just not all things."

"Interesting. I hadn't thought of that," said Father Tim. He was a very honest priest, and he rubbed his white and red bearded chin thoughtfully, turning his gaze out the window to the courtyard.

"So you're saying animals don't go to hell?" asked Nick.

73

He was sitting next to Phil, who seemed to agree with an almost imperceptible nod.

"We haven't even determined if there is a hell," said Father Tim. "We can't be sending cats and dogs and children off to a place that doesn't exist."

This was also common, a sort of circular reasoning that made us rethink everything we'd been talking about. Still, there were a few whispers in the room. Was a Catholic priest really telling us there was no hell?

Father Tim came forward and sat on the front edge of his desk, looking out at the quiet group. "I don't think God speaks to animals in the same way, and that makes us very special," he began. "Our conscience tells us when we're heading down the wrong path. Daisies, oak trees, ants, beetles, frogs, horses, and yes, even Mr. Bo Jangles and Clarisse, they're fundamentally different. They don't get to choose; only we have that privilege."

"But that still doesn't answer the question of hell," I said. "The Bible says it's there. Are you saying it's not?"

Father Tim jumped up and took three great strides to the chalkboard. He wrote down a Bible verse. When this happened it was assumed that everyone would take the many-translation Bibles from inside the desks and find the passage, which we all dutifully proceeded to do.

The verse was Colossians 1:20, which I found pretty fast because it's in the New Testament and I've got the order of books down cold in that thing.

By the time I'd read it and looked up, Father Tim had

written a total of eleven more verses on the white board and he was still going. I'd never seen him do this—none of us had—and Bible pages were flipping like crazy at every desk.

Philippians 2:10–11, Revelation 5:13, Hebrews 1:2, 1 Timothy 2:6, Ephesians 1:22, John 3:36, Titus 2:11, and on and on until the board was filled with verses and we all sat staring, not sure what we were supposed to do.

When Father Tim finally turned around, he looked as if he was winded by the effort and had to catch his breath. "I could go on," he said. "But I think these will begin to answer our question about heaven and hell and who's going where."

"Can you paraphrase?" asked Oh. "It's a little overwhelming."

Father Tim looked back at everyone looking at him and began reeling off the verses by heart. He ran them together without looking at the board, speaking in a voice that was growing in volume around every scriptural turn, as if the words had been written specifically for us to hear and he was the messenger. He ended in 1 Timothy with his hands out in the air, suspended on an invisible cross: "He gave himself as a ransom for *everything* and *everyone*."

A moment of silence followed as he stared at a perplexed room full of students.

"Are we going to be tested on this?" asked Ethan.

I'm sure everyone felt like laughing, but hardly anyone did.

"There are words in those verses that repeat and repeat," Father Tim answered. "But the message of these passages is easy to miss. People have been missing or hiding or ignoring this message for a long time. It's a shame how rarely we hear it, how much we try even to disguise it."

He looked directly at me, no one else, and I had a feeling then that no matter who else he addressed, the whole message was for me and me alone.

"Here is your answer, Oh: All creatures, all men and women, all children, all dogs and cats and flowers and mountains, *all* of them are saved. If that's not the truth, then I think the whole thing is probably a lie. Let's assume for a moment that you, Oh, do not choose God. Does this prevent Him from choosing you? I conclude, from these many verses, that it does not. Either He saves everyone or He saves no one."

It was radical stuff, for sure. Some good Catholic parents were bound to be up in arms. The school was broke and the priest had gone bananas.

I was beginning to wonder what Mr. Fielding had told Father Tim over the years. Did he know I might never die, might go on living forever, stuck on earth, unable to answer the question of hell for myself?

◆ ◆ ◆

"Later on, loser."

That's what Ethan said to me after school when he was done destroying me in front of a good number of people, jogging off the court to catch up with Marissa.

This is the part where I should have just smiled and walked away. A lot of what came after could have been avoided if I'd just kept my mouth shut. But I was feeling invincible, the idea of being indestructible taking hold in a way I didn't even understand at the time. It was making me say stupid things at stupid times.

"You know what your problem is?" I yelled. Ethan stopped on a dime, his wide shoulders turned, and he glared as if to dare me to open my trap again.

I hesitated and Ethan started walking toward me, tossing his racquet to Marissa for safekeeping.

"You gonna tell me my problem, or am I supposed to guess?"

"You're a total jerk, Ethan, simple as that."

Ethan kept coming toward me, smiling and shaking his head like I was some sort of brainless idiot.

"You feeling sorry for yourself because you got whipped?"

He was right up in my grill, breathing his lunch breath all over me.

"Or because that fake daddy of yours is gone?"

He had the swagger of an over-confident prize athlete without the knowledge of his first big injury.

"Take that back," I said.

"Nope, not gonna do it," said Ethan, his nose practically touching mine.

If it was true his punches couldn't hurt me, what was stopping me from rearranging the school bully's face right then and there?

"I'm telling you, Ethan, you better take that back. You don't know who you're messing with."

That did it. Ethan let out an attention-grabbing laugh and shoved me hard enough with both hands that I tripped and fell on the pavement.

A crowd started to gather to watch the blood start pouring.

"You really shouldn't have done that," said Milo. He knew the truth, knew that nothing Ethan could throw at me would help him now.

"How about you go fix your mascara and stay out of this?" Ethan said, glaring at Milo.

"Can't say I didn't warn you."

In the past I would have starting running for the hills, steering clear of the smell of danger, but I couldn't let it go. Something had changed inside me. I started moving toward him, fists clenched, and Ethan punched me about half speed in the gut, expecting me to buckle over and puke on my own shoes.

But I didn't feel a thing. "You'll have to do better than that."

And so he did, putting everything he had into a sucker punch so wild it's amazing he didn't miss my head altogether. He caught me in the ear hard enough to throw me off balance.

Two seconds later I was standing in front of him again, my own face moving fast into *his* grill. I grabbed him by the shoulders and cranked my forehead into his, our heads making a terrible sound like a watermelon dropped on the sidewalk. Ethan reeled back, shocked and confused, and the girls standing around gasped.

"Told you so," Milo chortled.

I watched the fragile rage build in Ethan's eyes. He glanced at the faces around him and saw he wasn't getting any support.

"Something's not right about this. You should be on your ass right now."

"Maybe so, or maybe you don't hit as hard as you thought."

"Forget about it." Ethan shrugged, trying to save face as he moved into a group of girls including Marissa. Normally they would have taken him in, if for no other reason than because he was popular. But this time everyone moved away, leaving Ethan standing alone four feet from where he'd been when he punched me.

Something about the unexpected circumstances must have set him to running his mouth off about things he'd obviously been saving for a more opportune time.

"You guys know this place is doomed, right? Father Tim is out of his mind. Holy Cross was already finished, but that sermon in class definitely takes the prize for stupid moves. It's like he *wants* the place to shut down. I'm just glad I'm jumping ship before the whole thing goes under."

"What are you saying?" I asked.

"We're all ending up at South Ridge anyway. Holy Cross

is broke. No money, no school. Where else does a plumber teach history? Are you *kidding* me?"

He shook his head and glanced at all the faces around him. Me, Milo, Nick, Phil, Oh, even Marissa and a couple other girls had gathered around to listen.

"Whatever." Ethan shrugged. "You guys wanna hang around this rat hole until it folds, that's your problem. I'm done."

He put an arm around Marissa's shoulder and she shook him off violently, shouting into his face, "Just go, then!"

She threw Ethan's tennis racquet into the parking lot. No one would look him in the eye as Marissa ran off with her two friends. There was no doubt about it now, the last great athlete at Holy Cross had been shamed in public by a jury of his peers. He was as good as gone.

"Surrounded by losers," said Ethan, shaking his head and laughing despite the fact that we all knew he'd been royally crushed. "I'll be sure and let everyone at South Ridge know only the gay dudes are left." He hurled a few more insults over his shoulder as he retreated for the parking lot in search of his one-hundred-twenty-dollar tennis racquet.

"Who knew he was such a devout Catholic?" Phil remarked. "I'm surprised he even *listened* to Father Tim in class today."

"His parents are loaded and *totally* Catholic," answered Nick. "If they pull the plug, Holy Cross might really be finished."

"You should have wiped the court with his face," Milo told me without a hint of sarcasm. "You're not going to get another chance."

"Neither are you," I reminded him. "And Oh's right. He's trouble. If we ever do end up at South Ridge, he'll have a price on our heads and it won't be cheap."

"Calm down," said Milo. "We're not going anywhere. And good riddance to that guy."

"Remember grade school?" Nick piped up as we all began walking back from the courts. "Ethan sucked at everything. We called him Gangler, remember that? Couldn't hit the broad side of a barn with a basketball, slow, clumsy—the guy was terrible. Remember?"

"That explains a lot," Oh said as we arrived at the midpoint between the gym and the parking lot. "You guys are so dense. He's a fighter, and just about the time he's mastered the game, everyone's moved on to something else. You gave him a target to shoot for: being a great athlete. Well, news flash, he's arrived. The only thing is, the target moved. Winning means everything to Ethan and nothing to you."

"He'll be better off with people who think the way he does," said Milo. "I'm glad he's leaving."

A breeze kicked up dead leaves at our feet.

"We're doomed if this place closes," said Phil. More than likely he was thinking about a group of giant, cocky athletes led by Ethan, finding him alone in the locker room.

◆ ◆ ◆

A half hour later we were at the batting cages—Milo's idea. We'd decided on several more tests that would escalate in danger as long as everything kept working. Oh had written down notes in a little notebook with a pink diamond-patterned cover on it.

"What do you think of argyle?" she asked us, flipping the cover back on its cheap metal spiral. Milo looked at her like she was nuts — (a) for being so random, and (b) because the thought of Milo in an argyle sweater was hilarious.

"Do I look like a preppy to you?" he asked, staring down at his black shirt, black jeans, black shoes.

"It doesn't mean what you think it does," said Oh with an expression that was fast becoming one of my favorites: Her nose widened with a smile, and her blond bangs fell over narrowed eyes. It was a mysterious look made for a smoke-filled room in a classic detective movie.

"Do we have to talk about this right now?" asked Milo. "Let's at least hit some balls."

Milo picked up a baseball bat and inserted four quarters into a slot. He pushed a speed button—slow—and walked to the plate, ready to take some swings.

"Okay, Oh, enlighten us already," said Milo, the first ball *thwooop*ing out of the machine and the sound of his bat cracking against it.

"It's a diamond mine, a famous one," said Oh.

"What is?" I asked.

"Argyle. It's why argyle sweaters are always made with a diamond pattern. That's what makes it an argyle."

Thwooop...crack!

"And here I thought it was the color schemes," said Milo. "I'm sure there's a reason you're telling us this...."

"The toughest material on earth is a diamond. The only way to cut one is by using another diamond."

"So does the pink have some secret meaning, too? Or is that just to match your cast?"

"It's the rarest color of diamond. The Argyle mine produces most of the pink diamonds on the planet. Plus, I like pink."

Oh turned the first page on her notepad toward us, where she'd penciled in the shape of a diamond and scribbled it full with pencil lead.

"It's a good symbol," she said.

"A good symbol for what?" asked Milo, stepping back from the plate and missing a ball as it clanged against the backstop.

I chimed in, half laughing despite the fact that obviously Oh was serious. "It's like a Batman symbol."

"More like a Joker card," said Milo, shaking his head and stepping back into the batters' box.

"Come on Milo, it's cool," said Oh. "This way we can talk in code, like 'pass me the diamond' or 'who has the diamond?' We need to be thinking about stuff like this, that's all I'm saying."

"She's got a point," I added, glad to be on Oh's side even if I did think the idea was basically ridiculous. I was anything but a superhero wearing a diamond on his chest.

Milo piped in. "As long as I don't have to wear pink argyle sweaters to be in your little club, I'm all good. Are we ready to do this thing or what? I've already wasted a buck. I'm not made of money."

"This will only take a second," said Oh. "Okay, here's what I have so far."

She held out her pad and revealed a penciled list. Each item in the list had a tiny diamond in front of it, like a bullet point. Her handwriting was a little on the round and swirly side, but thank God there were no hearts for dots or smiley faces. Oh's list:

- *Jacob has the ◆, which seems to make him invincible*
- *Don't know where it came from —*
- *Think it has something to do w/ Mr. Fielding*
- *Very little known about Mr. Fielding's past*
- *◆ appears to move when Jacob says YOU ARE INDESTRUCTIBLE*
- *This seems to be how Mr. F. gave ◆ to J*
- *J can pass ◆ to someone else if he looks at them & says the words*
- *When J gives ◆ away, he no longer has the power. it has moved.*

"Okay, I'm starting to like the diamond thing," said Milo. "It sort of weirdly works, you know what I mean?

84

Like passing the diamond to someone else is giving away something really valuable."

"And when Jacob takes it back, he's taking something valuable. He might be taking your life."

"Gee, thanks," I said. "No pressure or anything."

Oh smiled sweetly and flipped the page.

"Comes with the territory."

"As long as you don't make me wear a pink cape, I'm all good."

"What's this other list?" asked Milo, leaning in toward Oh more than I was comfortable with.

"This is all the stuff we don't know," she said. Milo glanced sideways at it.

"Long list. Looks like we've got some work to do."

- *Where did the ◇ come from & why did it choose J?*
- *Once J has given it to someone else, can they give it to another person?*
- *Should we keep it secret?*
- *Are we all in the same dream and just don't realize it?*
- *How much power do you have if you're holding the ◇?*
- *Is there anything that could kill you, or is it all powerful?*
- *Fire does nothing, but what about water? Could you still drown?*

- is there a Kryptonite?
- Can more than one person have the power at once, or is it really like one ✧, you either have it or you don't?
- Does the person have to be present in order for J to hand off the ✧ and to get it back?
- What is J not telling us?

"That last one is a real zinger," said Milo.

"I know," said Oh, looking at me and sniffling in the damp air. "But there has to be more you're not telling us. Didn't Mr. Fielding say *anything*? Weren't there any clues at all?"

A group of younger kids had ridden up and dropped their bikes loudly on the pavement. They ran to the opposite end of the cages and disappeared behind green mesh dividing each batter, arguing over who would go first.

I didn't know what to say. Sure, there was stuff I wasn't telling, but it was complicated.

"How about if we answer some of the other questions first," I said.

"Man of mystery," said Milo. "I can't compete with that."

She scanned the list and placed a thumb with clear nail polish against the fifth item on her list.

"Why did I know you were going to pick that one?" I asked.

"Because it's the most fun."

She had me there.

"I've got six quarters and three ones," I said after digging through my front pockets.

"Hand 'em over." Milo took all my money and pumped the dispenser full of coins, then pushed the "pro" button on the selector. I whistled. Pro meant ninety-mile-an-hour fastballs. There was a warning under the buttons that required hitters to use a helmet and removed any liability from the owners.

"Me first," said Oh.

"Dream on, sister," said Milo, standing next to home plate.

I pointed to the diamond-shaped home plate. "Did you plan this out?"

"Nope," she said. "It's fate."

Thwoop! The first of twenty balls flew by and practically blew Milo's hair back. If that's really how they pitched in the pros, batters were crazy to stand anywhere near home plate.

"You sure you want to do this?" I asked. Milo looked as stunned as I was and just stared at the machine, waiting for it to erupt and blast another scorcher past his face.

"Holy mother of God!" he screamed, plus a few other choice pronouncements I'd rather not repeat. It was exciting and terrifying at the same time, because we all knew the reason we'd come here, and it wasn't to watch baseballs hit the backstop.

I saw Oh out of the corner of my eye as she crept quietly closer to me. She spoke in a slow half-whisper.

"Give it to me."

I knew what she meant of course, but the words and the

look connected in my brain in a wholly inappropriate way, and I blushed like a seven-year-old who'd peed his pants on the playground.

Oh took my hand and stared at me, and without another word, licked her lips, and—

Thwoop!

"Damn that's fast!" screamed Milo.

I started to laugh and Oh squeezed my hand, drawing my gaze back to her. She leaned in, closed her eyes, and *almost* kissed me. I'd come within a hair of puckering up, which would have been über-embarassing. When she pulled back, her eyes opened slowly and I said the words. How could I deny a beautiful girl at a time like this? It was impossible.

"You are indestructible."

The pitching machine kept on pitching and she kissed me on the cheek, smiling as her lips pressed against my skin.

"This officially ends the competition for your affections," said Milo, who had turned to look at us. "It's my foul mouth, isn't it? That and the fact that I'm dead broke."

"You know I love you, Milo," said Oh affectionately. "And for the record, we're all broke. Now get out of the way."

She was gorgeous and fearless and I was in awe. She pulled her hair into a ponytail as the machine spit three more fastballs and Milo stepped out of her path.

"Test it first, before you go in there," I said.

"Punch me," she commanded Milo, but he wouldn't do it. Instead he kicked her in the shin hard enough to have hurt at least a little.

"Nothing."

"Are we really letting her do this?" asked Milo. "I mean, seriously, we're two guys and *she's* going in there?"

Before he could turn around, the sound of the pitching machine came again. Except this time, instead of ending with the clang of the backstop, we heard a sickening thump.

Oh had moved onto the diamond and taken the ball in the chest. The impact knocked her off her feet.

"Oh!" I yelled, starting toward her before I realized what I was doing. None of us were wearing helmets and only Oh was protected.

"Stay back!" she said, sitting up. "I'm totally fine! Didn't even fe—"

Her words were cut in half as another ball came hurling toward her. She was sitting up, and this time the blistering pitch smacked her in the forehead with a monstrous crack like the sound of a home-run swing.

Oh was lifted off the ground and landed like a rag doll against the backstop.

A quick shake of her head and she was smiling as the next pitch curved wide and missed her by a few inches.

"Get out of there, Oh! That's enough!" I screamed. But Oh was nothing if not thorough, and she positioned herself for another hit. Before the pitch could come, I grabbed her by the arm and pulled her to safety.

We looked up to see the group of kids down the way staring at us, slack-jawed.

"She's fine," Milo called out, trying to cover. "Wasn't as bad as it looked."

The kids started mumbling among themselves as I held Oh's head in my hands, searching for signs of madness.

"Are you absolutely sure you're okay?" It had been violent and not the least bit fun to watch someone get smashed in the head with a speeding baseball.

"If anything I feel even better than I did before we started. It was exhilarating."

I thought about the absurdity of both what she had said and what we were doing.

Oh took out her pink argyle notebook and began writing.

"We know you can still give it to someone else," she began, scribbling words I couldn't see as she explained, "and it was powerful enough to keep me from getting hurt even with a blow to the head."

"Girl, you'd be *dead* if it weren't for Jacob," said Milo, sounding moody. "And we don't know what's going to happen when you give it back."

"Sure we do," I said. "I took it back last time and she was fine. It'll be fine again."

"Yeah, but we can't know for sure it will keep working. You don't know—"

"I do know," I said. I heard the embarrassment in my own voice and saw that they knew, too.

"You took it back already, didn't you?" asked Oh, her eyes widening with surprise. I felt bad for jumping the gun, but it was like a little pet, this power I had. When I gave it away, it clawed to get back inside me.

"I didn't see any reason to wait once I pulled you to safety. I should have said something. Sorry."

"No, it's okay," said Oh. "It's great actually. We know it works."

"What are you writing down?" asked Milo.

"I've got a chart here with a column for each of us so we can keep track of everything we're doing individually. As far as I can tell it looks like this so far: Milo has avoided two minor injuries, one to his face and one to his thumb. Jacob has avoided death once, with the lamp at the store, and fire seems to have no effect on him. Me, I've been hit in the head hard enough to kill me and I feel fine, plus I was hit in the chest with a ninety-mile-an-hour fastball, also fine. And I did a face-plant on my longboard, no damage."

"God, I sound like a wimp," said Milo. "The next one is on me and that's final."

"Sounds like a plan," said Oh, checking her watch and returning the pad to her pocket. She sounded thrilled to keep going—*too* thrilled, it seemed to me.

As it turned out, she was at the exhilarating start of a deadly habit that would eventually eat us alive.

◆ ◆ ◆

When we left the batting cages, Milo was hungry and wanted to hit a taco van for buck-fifty burritos, but me and

Oh, we just wanted to drift through the neighborhood and talk about nothing in particular.

"Dudes, I *gotta* eat. How much you got?" Milo had asked.

I gave Milo my last dollar, which he put together with change from under his seat, and he took off on his own for afternoon sustenance.

Five minutes later I was alone with Oh in the endless maze of ranch-style houses, a canopy of damp tree limbs overhead that made the world feel heavy and private. We were on our own for the first time since we'd met.

"This is nice." Oh was gliding along the sidewalk on her longboard, holding on to my shoulder as I pulled her.

"You mean me pulling you or you and me alone?"

"Both," she answered, giving her board a kick and rolling out past me under the trees. Her long hair blew back in waves under her red cap. Oh turned and reached back toward me with her hand, the one with the pink cast, as she slowed down.

I smiled, relieved. "Be careful on that thing," I said, walking faster to catch up. When I got close enough so she could touch me, she moved up on the nose of the board and grabbed my hand.

"Let's ride together. You do the kicking."

I put one foot on the board, not a car in sight, a long stretch of sidewalk in front of us. There was a vision in my head of crashing and falling on top of her, rolling around on the grass in front of someone's house. Not the worst way to take a spill.

"Let's do this," I said, grabbing her around the waist and shoving off with three big kicks on the pavement. We were sailing. She laughed and grabbed my hands, wobbling on the board as she pulled me closer. When we slowed to a reasonably safe speed she turned in my direction.

This time, when she leaned in, she really did kiss me for the first time. No one was steering the ship we were on. It was a dangerous first kiss, an electric, adrenaline-inducing high I wished could stay with me for the rest of my life.

"Tell me more about Mr. Fielding," she said, our lips coming apart as the board slowed to a stop and I stepped off.

It felt almost like a trick. I kiss you, tell me your secrets. What could I tell her that wouldn't give too much away, remind me of how guilty I felt, or leave me choking back tears because I missed him so much?

"He had some money," I said, thinking this might be easiest. "Enough to keep me at Holy Cross. And he knew Father Tim for a while, like way before I met either one of them."

"What was his house like?"

This was actually a very perceptive question, because I'd lived there for a while but never talked about it, and I'd only been back there once since the accident.

"Well, for starters, it was small. Two bedrooms, a kitchen, a living room. He lived simply. Kind of beyond simple, if you want to know the truth. He preferred the outdoors and I know he traveled a lot before I came along. Plus he had this place at the coast where he kept a lot of his things. It's funny you mention it, because I went back to the house a few days after the accident, and I was reminded of how empty it was. Kind of mysterious, that part. It's hard to explain, but I kind of felt like he carried his whole self around with him. When he was with me, he was *really* with me, especially when we went out to breakfast together."

"What did you guys talk about when you went to breakfast?"

"I don't know, all kinds of stuff. We read the paper, took bites off each other's plates, talked about books, especially sci-fi and stuff like that. He knew a lot about history, kind of like Mr. Coffin. He was into escape artists, illusionists, stuff like that. We just, I don't know, talked about whatever came up."

Oh closed her eyes, holding my shoulder again and gliding along on her board.

"Sounds nice."

"How about you? You talk to your dad much?"

Oh opened her eyes and started to say something but stopped, and I decided not to push her about things with her parents. I got the feeling she didn't like talking about how it felt being from a broken family. Still, I felt a little robbed, like I'd given away too much without any payback.

"Come on!" she yelled back at me, smiling. "Let's do that kissing thing on the board again."

She didn't have to ask me twice.

TEN
DAYS TO
MIDNIGHT

THURSDAY, OCTOBER 11TH

I had just asked Oh out on a date in the lamest of all possible ways, and it didn't go quite as I'd planned.

Me: *There's something I want to show you.*

Oh: *Don't be gross.*

Me: *The coast isn't gross.*

Oh: *I don't get it.*

Me: *Will you go to the coast with me?*

Oh: *When?*

Not a no. A good sign.

Me: *Saturday.*

Oh: *Can't this weekend. have to stay with my dad. he pays for school, I visit. that's our deal.*

Me: *Saturday after?*

Oh: *Hang on.*

Seven minutes passed, but it seemed like seven hundred. I thought about how little I knew about Oh's past. Obviously I'd been too caught up in my infatuation to even ask if her parents were married or not. How did she even afford to attend Holy Cross?

Oh: *Mom said OK. how are we getting there?*

Me: *Got it covered.*

Oh: *Take Milo? is he driving?*

Ugh. Take Milo? What the heck for? I didn't know how to respond, so I didn't respond at all.

Five minutes later:

Oh: *We don't have to take him if you don't want to.*

Oh: *Does what you need to show me have to do with you know what?*

Me: *Yes.*

Oh: *Then I take it back. we need to take Milo with us.*

Me: *OK.*

Two minutes of dead air.

Oh: *Is this a date?*

Me: *Guess so.*

Oh: *So you want to date me.*

Me: *You kissed me first.*

Oh: *You make me feel safe.*

Another two minutes of dead air, and then Oh sent me a question I couldn't answer.

Oh: *What are you going to show me?*

I ignored the message and rolled out of bed to a symphony of three retired priests getting ready for the day—hacking up phlegm, farting, blowing their noses in the shower. Ten days in the church house had helped me realize there was at least one consequence to never getting married: a high risk of becoming oblivious to your own gargantuan annoyances.

My turn came up in the shower, and I double-checked for hairs and snot before stepping in and letting the warm water rush over my head. I thought about everything we'd done. We'd already tested fire, falling, sharp objects, electric shock, and being leveled with a ninety-mile-an-hour fastball. Oh insisted we needed to try at least two more things before we could be certain of what I could do with the power, but first we had to get through another day at Holy Cross.

At least Ethan wouldn't be there to bug us. I figured that out the moment I stepped on campus because it was all anyone was talking about. There was a rumor floating around that his dad had called Father Tim and "ripped him a new one," as Nick put it.

I drifted through the morning classes with Mr. Beck and Miss Pines, thinking mostly about the fact that my first real date with Oh was going to include my best friend. It was sure to be awkward, especially since I'm almost positive he had been making a play for her before I entered the picture.

But I suppose Oh had a point. There was something I knew about—or at least thought I knew, if dreams and half-remembered memories were any indication—that they both deserved to know. I wasn't even sure what *it* was, only that it was there.

Seven days ago, a full week after Mr. Fielding's death, I lurched awake in the church house. I don't think I'd had so much a dream as a broken memory of a brief conversation between me and Mr. Fielding. I played it back, alone there in the dark.

"If something happens to me and you don't know what to do, come back here, okay?"

I was like, okay, what for?

He'd looked in a certain direction, in a certain place, my eager eyes following his, and then he'd completely changed course.

"Let's go get some chowder and walk on the beach. It's a hell of a day out there."

◆　◆　◆

After our initiation at the batting cages, the testing didn't bother us so much. It was like playing a violent video game or watching a war movie. After a while none of it seemed real anymore. It was shocking how quickly we became desensitized. Like nothing we were doing would have any consequences.

"We have to figure out if you can give it to anyone you want, not just people you like," said Milo as the three of us sat eating in the courtyard. "And whether it can be passed on from there. So, like, can you give it to me and then can I give it to someone else?"

"You're assuming I like you," I answered dryly.

Milo was eating a bowl of cold mac and cheese left over from the night before. For some reason he found it necessary to jam the metal fork into my arm, where it stuck in my skin. I started screaming like a stuck pig and Milo freaked out, apologizing as he pulled the fork out. When he realized I'd only been kidding, he wrestled me to the ground and dug his chin into my chest. Even in my indestructible state, he was impossible to beat in a wrestling match.

"Will you two quit screwing around? Milo is right," said Oh. We both looked up, hair disheveled and dirt on our jackets like two grade-school kids having it out over a donut. "We could test it right now, if you want."

Oh had that mischievous, smoky-eyed look on her face as she bit into an apple. Milo and I returned to the stone bench to hear her latest plan.

"We haven't found anything like Kryptonite yet, nothing that you can't overcome when you've got it. As long as you're covered, it appears that nothing can harm you. We haven't tested drowning or a really far fall yet, but other than that it's looking like a person really is impossible to injure when they have it."

"We haven't tried shooting each other," said Milo.

"Thank you for that unfortunate reminder," Oh responded.

"Actually, I can verify the gun thing," I admitted sheepishly.

Both Oh and Milo stared at me with jaw-dropping expressions. They were, I think, stunned into silence.

"It takes a surprising amount of nerve to shoot yourself in the foot. I almost couldn't do it."

"Oh my God, Jacob, tell me," Oh demanded, leaning in closer.

I explained that the priests kept a grand total of one gun on the church house grounds, an old shotgun they used "on rare occasion" to scare off crows when they got too thick.

"Priests make their own rules," said Milo. "You guys ever notice that?"

"I got up really early this morning, like before dawn, and stood barefooted in the back forty. Like I said, I almost couldn't go through with it."

"But you did." Oh was mesmerized; she was enjoying this a little more than I was comfortable with.

"Two of the old guys came out and I said I'd scared off a whole slew of crows, but dang, they were mad. Mostly because I woke them up."

"So how did it feel? Can I see?" asked Oh. Milo just sat there shaking his head.

"I can't believe you shot yourself in the foot."

After I peeled off my shoe and my sock and showed them both that my foot was unharmed, Milo asked what it had felt like.

"Not much, a little pressure maybe."

"Unbelievable," Oh concluded.

"What about a chainsaw?" Milo asked, leaning back as I put my sock back on.

"You're a sick puppy," Oh scolded.

"No, seriously though. If I tried to cut my arm off with a chainsaw, what would happen?"

"I don't think that's different enough from Oh's crash on the board. The pavement pretty much acted like a chainsaw would on her skin. Her skin should have shredded, but nothing happened."

"I can't believe we're having this conversation."

"Okay, one more, just indulge me." Milo had obviously given this a lot of thought.

"What about getting sick? If Jacob kept the power and never gave it away, could he get, like, cancer? Could he even get a cold?"

"I don't know how we'd figure that one out," I said. "Some of this stuff we're going to have to decide for ourselves or just cross the bridges when we come to them."

"Let's just hope we never cross a bridge and find a guy with a chainsaw waiting for us on the other side," said Oh, shaking her head. "Let's focus on something we can actually test."

She tapped her pencil in the pink diamond notebook, then took the same pencil and stuck it inside her cast, itching a piece of skin I couldn't see.

"Is that thing even doing any good?" asked Milo.

Since the spill on the longboard, the cast looked a lot less sturdy.

"It's keeping you from sticking me in the arm with a fork," she said. "Just shut up for one second and listen to me."

"Okay, okay—I'm all ears."

Oh rolled her eyes and went back to her list as Milo took a bite of cold mac and cheese.

"You do realize that fork was in my arm," I said.

"Jacob," said Oh. "Zip it."

I nodded. "Zipping it, no problem."

"It also looks like only one person can have it at a time, but one thing we don't know is whether or not Jacob has to be present in order to pass the power to someone else. That's a big one, especially if we're going to help as many people as possible."

"What are you talking about?" asked Milo. "Who said anything about helping people?"

Oh kept itching the inside of her cast with the pencil as she went on.

"I know, it's a real thrill trying to kill each other, I get it," she said. "But don't you think we need to put it to practical use at some point? I bet that's what Mr. Fielding did. I bet he was this mild-mannered, outdoorsy guy by day, but actually used this power to save a lot of people."

"I don't know," I said, the runner inside me lurching away from the kind of responsibility Oh was hinting at. "I never imagined him doing anything like that. I'm pretty sure I would have sensed that something odd was going on." I paused. "I guess we did end up talking about comic books and superheroes a few times. And he had this weird fascination with magicians I'd never even heard of. The Fire King, Harry Kellar, Alexander Herrmann, strange dudes who did even stranger stuff."

"Did you ever think this power you have might be somehow connected to magic? I mean, we don't have a lot to go on here. You should think about stuff like that."

I shrugged. Magic wasn't real, it was an illusion, and Mr. Fielding's interest in it was never anything serious. What we were experiencing was like the opposite of magic, not an illusion at all, but real power from a real source.

"Just tell me this much," she prodded. "Is there anything you can think of that might get one of us hurt? Some sort of rule we don't know about?"

"I don't know about any rules," I said.

Oh categorized my answer as "not very helpful," but she smiled delightfully from the corner of her mouth, shaking her head and looking at me with those beautiful eyes.

"I can't believe you shot yourself in the foot."

I shrugged. "I'm not always a clear thinker before dawn."

"I'll tell you one thing," Milo jumped in, wiping the corners of his cheese-laden mouth. "Number two on your list: Should we keep it secret? Absolutely. Anyone finds out and it's straight to CIA headquarters for all of us. Lots of needles and when it's all over they use Jacob as a military weapon. To hell with that."

"You're nuts, but probably right," I said. "We have to keep it secret no matter what."

"Luckily no one would believe us anyway," said Oh.

"One thing we can test right now is whether or not Jacob can protect someone he doesn't care about," said Milo. "We know he likes you." He nodded in Oh's general direction.

"Yeah, a lot more than he likes *you*," said Oh. It didn't look like Milo appreciated the joke very much.

"That's debatable," said Milo.

"Is not," said Oh.

She leaned in and put her pink cast against my cheek, kissing me quickly on the lips.

"That's incredibly unfair. If we were gay you'd be up a creek without a paddle. You wouldn't even be in the game."

"He's right, you know," I said.

"Aw. You guys are having a bromance. That's really cute."

"How about we just agree that I like you both the same," I said. Before they could keep baiting each other, I continued, "Out of all the girls in this school, the one that I care about the least has got to be Emily. She plays head games with guys like Nick and Phil."

"Perfect," said Oh. "She's sitting right over there with the rest of her posse. See if you can slip her the diamond."

"That sounded all wrong," I said.

"Lunch is almost over. Just do it," she urged.

"Okay, okay—don't rush me," I said, sighing. I wondered if I would ever get it back and felt a heaviness in my gut as if something were hunkering down, hoping not to be disturbed. I looked at Emily, said the words, and waited. I imagined a black beast leaving my body, hovering around me and wanting back in, then dutifully floating away and disappearing into Emily's lithe body.

"How about putting that fork to good use, Milo?" asked Oh. "Go work your magic on the ladies' club."

Milo had been going to school with these girls since kindergarten. He didn't have the slightest problem making small talk. I watched as he approached them, fork in hand, and sat down sideways on the plastic chair next to Emily. We couldn't really see what he was doing, other than making all the girls laugh about something.

Then, he turned to me and mouthed: *Give it to me.* I took it back from Emily, thought the words, and now Milo had the power.

Everything seemed to be going fine until Marissa screamed. She looked at Milo like he had just snapped her bra and slapped him across the face. She got up and stormed off, followed by Mary, June, and Emily.

"That didn't look good," I said. "I guess we've got some limitations after all."

When Milo arrived, he was incensed.

"Thanks a lot, Oh. It's not bad enough I have to be the third wheel with you two, now every girl in school thinks I'm an idiot."

"What did you do, grab her boob?" I joked. Oh started

laughing. She had a certain laugh that would not be denied—you either joined in or left the premises—and Milo couldn't stop himself from cracking a smile.

"You can check one more item off your list."

Oh and I looked at each other, then back at Milo for an explanation.

"I poked Emily as hard as I could. Nothing, nada—she didn't even notice," he said, holding up the fork. "Then, when you gave me the signal that I had it, I said the words in my head—*you are indestructible*—looking right at Marissa. Then I tried the same thing on her."

Oh started flipping pages in her pink diamond booklet until she came to the checklist.

"It looks like it can't go more than one person past you, Jake-o. One degree of separation, that's all we get."

Oh scribbled in her notebook as she talked. "Jacob to Milo, yes; Milo to Marissa, no."

"I don't think I'd keep eating mac and cheese with that thing," I said, looking at the fork in Milo's hand.

Milo shrugged, digging into his plastic bowl for one last bite. "I probably shouldn't have risked it. Ten to one she's on her cell talking to Ethan right now, telling him how I stuck a fork in her ass. That's not likely to go over very well."

"Yeah, good old Marissa. She can't stay mad at Ethan. This'll just give her an excuse to get him even more riled up."

Milo downed the last bite of his lunch and shook his head.

"I've stabbed two people with a fork today. What's wrong with me?"

Oh was making some final notes on the pad as she said "Get it back" without looking up.

"Already did," I said slyly.

"You are so crafty, Jacob Fielding. What's going on in that head of yours?"

If I'd told her the truth—that I couldn't bear to part with the power for very long without feeling like it would claw me to death trying to get back inside—she probably wouldn't have been so cavalier.

The lunch bell rang and we agreed to do one last test after school, then meet at the loft at Coffin Books to do some studying. Oh said she had a plan, and that if the last test went as she expected it to, things were about to get really interesting.

◆　◆　◆

"You ready?" I asked. I rarely used my cell phone to call anyone but I felt an overwhelming desire to hear Oh's voice.

Milo and I were standing at the edge of the woods, barely in the parking lot, letting a soft drizzle wet our hair for reasons I can't begin to explain. Something about living in Oregon has made us prefer the feeling of slight dampness on our skin.

"Still on my board," answered Oh. It sounded like she was out of breath from making the ten-block longboard journey from Holy Cross to her apartment.

"Are you close?" I asked.

"Yeah, I'm pulling into the parking lot now. Give me a couple of minutes to find a hammer." Oh hung up while I was still talking, and I turned to Milo.

"She needs five more minutes and we're good to go."

"Have you already forked over the diamond?"

"Nope," I answered, not the least bit interested in letting it go if I didn't have to. I wasn't telling Milo or Oh, but it was getting harder to transfer the power every time I did it. Something about it felt wrong, like I wasn't supposed to be doing it to begin with, like whatever it was didn't want out. And that was only the half of it. The clawing or biting—I didn't even know what to call it—it was getting stronger when it tried to get back in, too.

We checked our phones every minute or so, pacing in the parking lot scattered with cars and wondering what was taking so long. Some students were playing tennis around the front of the school, but other than that, Holy Cross was a quiet place on a Thursday afternoon.

"How long does it take to find a hammer?" asked Milo. "She should just use a book or something."

The test was simple: Could I transfer the power from a long distance and then get it back again? If the test worked then it would open up a world of possibility. I could protect anyone I wanted to. Heck, I could protect the president if I wanted.

Oh was planning to hit herself with a hammer. Not too dangerous and fast to boot, just the kind of test we needed.

"Tell her to hit herself with a frying pan," said Milo. "I'm dying for some chow and this is getting seriously boring."

My phone buzzed.

Okay. I'm ready.

I hesitated, my thumbs hovering ghostlike over the keyboard.

"Did I mention I'm hungry? Just send it over already," said Milo.

And so I did, closing my eyes and envisioning Oh smiling just so, her bangs hanging loose over her eyes.

We wanted to make sure that the power was able to transfer to someone without actually speaking to the person, so I texted her back instead of calling.

You got it.

A minute later she hadn't replied. "Call her," Milo demanded, stepping around to the other side of his car and opening his door. He looked down the long driveway to the street beyond, and it was all I could do not to wrench the power back into myself. It was lurking outside in the world, searching for a way back in.

"Someone's coming," said Milo. I followed his gaze.

"That's not *someone*, it's Ethan."

"Is she done? Can you get it back? I think it might come in handy about now."

Still no text from Oh. I tapped out her number and held the phone to my ear as the two-tone MINI Cooper came closer. It was a car I would have liked had it not been owned by a guy I couldn't stand.

Oh picked up just about the time Ethan revved the engine of the little car, munching old pavement into gravel in its path.

"You done?" I asked.

"No! You need to let me keep it."

It wasn't a request, it was an order, like she was in control.

"Is everything okay over there? What's happening?"

"Just don't take it back yet. Give me a little more time. I need to do one more thing."

Ethan had come within a few feet of Milo's crummy Geo Metro and slammed on the brakes, sliding sideways and coming to a stop without a lot of room for error. I had to hand it to Ethan, the guy could drive.

"Milo Coffin, you nearly jumped out of your bra!" he howled, stepping out of the MINI Cooper.

"I have to take it back," I said into the phone. But Oh was gone. She'd hung up without answering, and I had no idea what she was up to. For all I knew, she was about to step in front of a bus.

Ethan had a new haircut, a phohawk that was shaved on the sides and came up in the middle of his head in an upside-down V. He wasn't alone. Marissa climbed out of the backseat, and Reginald Boone stepped out on the passenger side. Boone was part of an earlier wave of defectors to South Ridge (no one I knew ever called him Reginald or Reggie). A big dude, more fat than muscle but plenty of both, without much interest in anything but girls and beer. He was a starting linebacker on the South Ridge football team.

Boone stood in front of the car with an air of total boredom. He looked at Ethan, then back at me, shaking his head.

"Why you gotta always be causing problems?"

At the beginning of the school year, when Boone was still a Holy Crosser, I'd tested my backhand in the locker room and accidentally cracked him on the side of the head with my racquet.

"I'm not the one making trouble," I answered, a subtle tip of the chin in Ethan's direction.

Milo said something about how Ethan and Marissa deserved each other, and before we knew it we were staring up at two large football players who'd moved within striking distance of our faces.

"Take it easy," I said. We didn't have the power, and I could tell Milo was perilously close to throwing a punch or saying something that might get one thrown at *us*.

"You talking to me or your boyfriend here?" asked Boone.

It seemed that Ethan was surveying the situation, wondering how it would go down if things turned violent after what had happened at the tennis court. He needed to impress his new teammate and the girl standing behind him, but he'd tried to take me down before and failed.

"You looking for another whipping?" asked Milo. Even with the boots he was staring *way* up into Ethan's face. I knew what Milo was thinking—that I'd give him the power and he'd have his moment.

Ethan shoved Milo hard with both hands, but Milo didn't go down. He looked at me expectantly and I could almost read his mind. *Come on man, you got your shot, give me mine!*

I slid my phone open and started texting Oh as fast as I could, but Boone grabbed it out of my hand.

"This your new friend, the skater?" he asked. I lurched forward to take it back as Boone turned away from me. "I bet she's a real pig on wheels."

"Actually, she's pretty hot," Ethan said, wincing as soon as the words left his mouth. He was no doubt imagining what we saw, which was Marissa's expression of disgust. Seeing the error of her ways, she threw up her hands and made a prissy *uuuuhhh!* sound that went on way too long. It was an ugly sound from a pretty girl. She stormed off, crossing paths on the sidewalk with Mr. Bo Jangles, who meowed loudly and reeled back as if to pounce on her leg.

"Shut up, you brainless cat!"

"Now look what you've made me do," said Ethan, turning back to Milo, who was all clenched fists as he looked up into the face of a suddenly very serious guy with a big size advantage.

"I think your new girl is really going to like your text," said Boone, sliding my phone shut and tossing it back at me.

Milo glanced at me for a split second, and I nodded

softly. Oh *had* to be out of harm's way by now, and I'd taken the power back. Unfortunately for Ethan, I'd transferred it to my best friend.

"I tell you what I'll do," said Milo, folding his arms in front of his chest, loving every second of power over his opponent. "I'll let you have one free shot, right in the face. But if I'm still standing, I get one in your nuts."

Boone laughed and shoved Ethan playfully. "Dude, you gotta take that deal. It's too sweet."

"You're serious?" said Ethan.

"Hell, yeah, I'm serious. You chicken?" asked Milo.

"Let it go," I said, hoping to get Milo to calm down. "Let's just get out of here and forget this ever happened."

Ethan's blow came out of nowhere, and it was way bigger than any of us expected. My guess is he wanted to make sure it worked this time.

The punch waylaid Milo, sending him swinging backward like a jack-in-the-box on a spring, but he didn't fall over. Ethan shook the sting out of his hand as Milo leaned way back, absorbing the vicious blow, then popped straight up again and shook the cobwebs from his head.

"That all you got?" asked Milo. "Mr. Bo Jangles punches harder than that."

"What the...?" Boone's words trailed off. He looked at Ethan and Milo and tried to decide if Ethan punched like a seven-year-old or if Milo was the toughest little bastard he'd ever seen.

Ethan was flustered. He must have been thinking about the

ragging he'd take at school the next day as he slapped Milo's face harder than I'd ever seen anyone hit a guy before.

Milo flew off his feet and landed in a pile on the pavement. He turned, a maniacal grin on his face, and stood back up.

"Nice try," he said, lifting his foot with alarming speed where it connected with a thud between Ethan's legs. Ethan went down hard and fast, curled into a ball.

"I don't know what the hell just happened, but something's not right," grumbled Boone. "No way Milo is that tough. *No* way!"

"Take a shot," dared Milo. "Go ahead! Let's see it!"

Boone looked at Milo standing his ground and was clearly tempted. This was a big guy, confused into inaction. I stepped in front of my best friend and stared at him, hoping I wouldn't get sucker punched from behind.

"I took it back," I told Milo. He glared at me with white fear in his eyes at the thought of getting ambushed by Reginald Boone.

"Took what back?" asked Boone. "What's with you knobs?"

Ethan was up on his feet again, hobbling toward the car, and—fortunately for Milo—Boone decided to follow him. Once inside the car, Ethan leaned out the window and puked on the wet pavement.

When his head came up, his eyes were narrowed with hate behind the windshield. I knew then that we'd made a horrible mistake. Ethan wasn't just an annoying former classmate anymore. Ethan was now our enemy, and it appeared that he had at least one powerful ally.

"I think that's going to come back to haunt us," I said as the MINI Cooper rolled into gear and raced down the drive toward the street.

"Yeah, but it might have been worth it. Did you see his face after he clobbered me the first time? He's scared."

"Milo, use your head, will you? Those two think you can take a punch like a rhino, but we both know that's not true. If Boone punches you like that for real, you're in deep trouble. Or worse, maybe they'll bring a baseball bat next time."

"I guess you're right," Milo admitted.

True terror is knowing you're getting beaten up at some point in the very near future.

My phone vibrated, and I opened it up, where I found two messages from Oh. The first one was a few minutes old and scared me.

Rode my board off roof of building. always wanted to do that. pavement taste = bad. but I'm fine.

"She's crazy," I whispered.

"Yeah, but you're in love," said Milo, putting a hand on my shoulder. "Not a thing you can do about it."

I imagined her gliding down the steep slope of the apartment roof, riding the board until it fell out from under her feet. If Oh had hesitated a minute longer, she probably wouldn't be alive to send me a text.

One minute had mattered a lot more than I thought a minute could.

The second message from Oh helped me understand what Boone had texted her when he'd grabbed my phone.

Since when is my butt bigger than Texas? thanks a lot.

I read it to Milo and he shook his head. We both laughed halfheartedly, got in his beat-up old car, and went in search of a pretty girl with pavement breath.

♦ ♦ ♦

On our way to pick up Oh, she called and said her mom was coming home early to take her shopping at the mall for new pants and a slice of pizza. Milo thought it sounded absurd at a time like this, but she argued that we needed to keep playing the roles of mild-mannered small-town kids.

"My mom is nosy," she had said. "Trust me; we don't want her sniffing around. Pick me up after, in front of the mall at like six. And bring your backpacks. She's going to want to see them."

At the time it had sounded juvenile, like we were still in middle school and had to prove to our parents that we were hard at it grinding out a paper or studying for a midterm. But meeting Ms. James taught me something quick: She kept a close eye on her one daughter.

Oh and her mom had the same eyes and the same California skin that didn't fit with the cloud-covered drizzle of the northwest. She went so far as to open the car door for Oh and then step in before her and sit down next to Milo.

"This a taxi?" she asked.

"No, ma'am. He just likes sitting in the backseat. He's funny that way," Milo said.

"Mm-hmmmm," she continued, running the palm of her hand along the cracked dashboard of Milo's car. She glanced at me and Milo, inspected the Taco Bell wrappers on the floor beneath her feet, and checked how much gas Milo had in the tank while Oh stood outside looking embarrassed.

Ms. James's gaze settled on me in the backseat, and I knew by the look on her face that I was dead if anything happened to her daughter. "Don't do anything stupid."

It was the last thing she said, followed by a narrow-eyed look that more than matched the blistering stare of her daughter. We would do something reckless at our own peril.

Oh got in, exasperated, and we waved to her mom as Milo pulled away from the curb.

"You weren't kidding about her," said Milo.

"Yeah, well, we've been through a lot together. She's protective."

I wanted to lay into her about her wild behavior earlier in the day, but when she turned to look at me, I couldn't do it. Her simmering smile disarmed me, and we were already downtown. Five or six blocks and we'd be at the loft. Better to wait until we were safely tucked away inside Coffin Books.

◆　◆　◆

"Looks like my dad is still here," Milo said. We'd entered Coffin Books and closed the door behind us, hearing someone moving around in the private office where we couldn't see.

"How do you know it's him?" asked Oh. "It could be anyone. Maybe it's an ax murderer."

"He does keep axes in there," said Milo. "And hammers."

"Stop that," said Oh.

Mr. Coffin stepped into the main part of the store, casting blurry shadows on the shelves of books. His silhouette looked like a bigger, slightly stooped version of Milo.

"Hey, Dad!" yelled Milo.

At the sound of Milo's voice, Mr. Coffin practically dove back into his office like a startled cat. Some sort of "Jeez! What the!" came out of his mouth and then, seeing it was us, he breathed a sigh of relief.

"Thanks for the warning." He looked like a barrel-chested gorilla in the shadowy light, all two hundred stocky pounds of him on the approach.

" 'Hey, Dad' seemed to cover it," said Milo.

Mr. Coffin took on a different appearance as he emerged from the darkened recesses of the bookstore. He had black hair, balding on top, and a five o'clock shadow that made you almost positive his back was covered with fur. I liked Mr. Coffin—a very friendly guy—but I kept thinking, *Milo, this is your future. You better get married quick.*

"You finished picking on your old man?" asked Mr. Coffin.

"Maybe."

Mr. Coffin glanced past me, and Oh reached out her hand, stepping forward.

"Pleased to meet you, Mr. Coffin. I love your store. And your unusual name."

Mr. Coffin shook her hand pleasantly.

"Bill's not that unusual, but thank you."

"Very funny, Dad."

Mr. Coffin looked at Milo with a raised eyebrow that said, *What? I'm not charming enough for your friends?*

"It's a long story, the last name."

"She knows," said Milo. "Already got her up to speed."

Mr. Coffin shrugged, but looked like he wished he could have told Oh the story of his last name himself. Then he turned his attention to me.

"Holding up?"

I frowned, shrugged. "Yeah, holding up."

He looked at Oh and Milo.

"You two go ahead. Couple new arrivals I want to show Jacob, strictly sci-fi super fan stuff." Mr. Coffin had a gift for hunting down obscure and out-of-print stuff and totally got off on sharing his latest finds.

Milo was more than happy to be free of his dad's presence and moved off toward the loft with Oh trailing behind.

"It was nice to finally meet you," said Oh, looking back as she walked away.

"Have a look around. First book's on me." Mr. Coffin really knew how to charm the new customers.

"He got the story of our name wrong, I'm sure of it," he then mumbled.

"What does it matter?" I asked.

"A guy changes his last name, it's a big deal."

The story wasn't actually all that complicated. It would be hard for Milo to screw it up. Bill Coffin *was* William Coflyn, but when they got into the scary book business, he named the store and dropped the *L*. Cofyn wasn't quite right, but Coffin was perfect. He didn't get out that much, so I'm not sure that many people even knew he'd ever changed it.

"I killed the name, you know?" he said.

"Huh?"

"I killed it. Only child and my folks are both dead. I was the last Coflyn."

This was getting awkward.

"Is there something you wanted to show me, Mr. C?"

Mr. Coffin pulled me into the sci-fi section, down a narrow row where it was darker and the sound of our voices was crushed by a million dense and dusty pages. He rubbed the stubble on his chin, a nervous habit, but his eccentricities didn't really bother me.

"It was a nice funeral." Mr. Coffin coughed. "I mean, as nice as something like that can be."

"Thank you for being there. He'd have appreciated that."

It was the last time we'd seen each other, and we hadn't talked much at the graveyard service.

"Not a lot of folks at the funeral," said Mr. Coffin. "That surprise you at all?"

I didn't know what to say. "I guess not. He was a private person, kind of like you."

Mr. Coffin nodded his agreement, leaned a hand against a row of paperbacks.

"Listen, Jacob, I feel I haven't been completely honest with you."

"About what?"

He looked toward the loft, making sure we were alone, I guess.

"I knew Mr. Fielding for a while, you know that, right?"

"Sure I know. So what?"

"Did he tell you anything about the work I did for him? Ever mention that?"

"You mean like finding books and stuff? He mentioned it once in a while."

"I looked for more than just books."

We both heard Milo yelling at me from the loft to get my butt up there. Mr. Coffin put his hand on my shoulder, trying to hold my attention a little longer.

"Um...okay." I was starting to feel uncomfortable again. "What else did you look for?"

"Look, Jacob, there's a certain kind of person I tend to attract. Collectors, people with a lot of interest in, you know..." He waved his hand over the store. "All this kind of stuff."

I couldn't see much from the corner where we stood, but I knew what he meant: strange theater props and posters, and the even more bizarre stuff hidden in the Coffin basement.

"And...?"

"And Mr. Fielding was the most curious guy I ever met. Deep pockets, too. Always looking for very specific kinds of items from certain dates, and not always books."

I had always known the two of them talked. Even when I'd met Milo at the store the first time, before Holy Cross, Mr. Fielding and Mr. Coffin had hunkered down together. I'd never given it a second thought, figuring they were just chatting about books they were reading.

"He didn't want me saying anything to you or anyone else," said Mr. Coffin.

"Jacob! Get your sorry ass up here!" Milo yelled.

"Just start without me," I yelled back. "Almost done."

"Whatever," a softer but more irritated Milo answered.

"What are you not telling me?" I asked Mr. Coffin.

He hesitated, leaning in a little closer. "Some of the things I found for him? They were kind of, I don't know, unusual, I guess."

"How do you mean?"

"Notes and drawings and artifacts relating to magicians, props for tricks that were ultimately too dangerous or didn't work like they were supposed to, stuff that never saw the light of day. Things that circulate in a very small circle of collectors."

I was beginning to have a feeling about where some of

these things might be and even what many of them were, but I didn't let on.

"There's one item I found that he wouldn't let me keep for him," said Mr. Coffin. "Paid me a lot of money for finding it. I'll be damned if I ever got to read it myself."

"A book?" I asked.

"Not sure, maybe. Or possibly a story. Either way it was in a locked box and I didn't have a key. I would have busted it open, but then Mr. Fielding wouldn't have paid me. He made that pretty clear."

I was starting to understand Mr. Coffin had motivations of his own.

"You want it back, and you think I know where it is. Is that it?" I asked.

"No. I don't want to keep it. I just want to see what was inside."

"Jacob! Get—your—ass—UP HERE!"

"They can't do the homework without me," I lied. "Let me think about this, okay? Maybe I can figure out where he put this box."

I started for the loft and Mr. Coffin grabbed my arm so hard that it scared me.

"That priest knows some things," he said. "He might know where to find it."

I pulled my arm free and started walking away. Father Tim? The connections were starting to fire in my head. Father Tim, Mr. Coffin, Mr. Fielding.

I was beginning to see that a lot had already been happening before I came on the scene.

◆ ◆ ◆

"All I'm saying is what if our timing had been off? We'd be driving to your funeral."

I arrived in the loft to find Milo and Oh fighting. Mr. Coffin had already yelled up to us, leaving the bookstore and locking up on his way out. We were alone, the three of us, free to talk in peace.

"At least I didn't smash my thumb."

"That's not funny."

"Not even a little bit?"

"No, not even a little bit. This whole thing is getting way out of hand. You could have been killed, Oh. How do you think that makes us feel?"

"Milo is right," I added, Oh's eyes darting between the two of us.

"I told you it was a mistake. I'm not going to do it again."

"Why do I find that hard to believe?" I asked. My encounter with Mr. Coffin had put me in a defensive mood.

"Are you saying you don't trust me?"

"No...yes... I guess I don't know. The thing with Ethan and Boone was scary. The two of them together are a time bomb waiting to go off. They're curious and they're jerks. Not a good combo."

"Then don't give it to me anymore. I don't need it."

"Cool it, you two," said Milo. "I can't handle any more broken furniture in this place. My mom already gave me a load of grief over that lamp."

"None of this matters, you guys," Oh said. "Don't you see? We've got something amazing and now we know the rules that govern it."

This was becoming a habit of Oh's: taking ownership of something that was mine.

"And better yet, I don't think this power has a Kryptonite. At least I can't find one."

"We haven't tried drowning," I said.

"That's not exactly true," said Oh, a little embarrassed.

"You did not," said Milo, staring her down until he caught her eye and knew she was telling the truth. "Unbelievable. You're out of control. *Totally* out of control."

I just shook my head, dumbfounded.

"It wasn't even dangerous. I did it in the kitchen at home."

Oh explained that she'd never gone looking for a hammer. Instead she had filled the sink with water and dunked her head all the way under.

"I sucked in a deep breath while I was under and figured if it didn't work the worst thing that would happen would be a lot of coughing and spitting. But nothing happened. I don't know if I was breathing water or not. I thought I was, but maybe it was like a dream or something. All I know is I stayed under trying to breathe for at least a couple of minutes and nothing happened."

"You see? There it is again," I complained bitterly. "What if I had taken it away when you were blissfully trying to breathe water? What then?"

"But you didn't." Her voice was at once pleading and apologetic. "I'm sorry, Jacob. I really am. I'm not going to do anything like that again. We don't need to take any more unnecessary risks, honest."

"We didn't need to take the ones we've already taken," I corrected. "This whole thing is leading nowhere good, I can tell you that." I sounded like someone's father. But everything about my life felt dangerous and out of control.

We sat in silence. I was pushing Oh away. I could see it in the way her shoulders slumped and she retreated to her pink pad, making notes as she so often did. I thought about the Pandora's box I'd opened up by simply writing three words on Oh's pink cast.

But it would take a lot more than my scolding for Oh to change her mind. She stood up and laid out a plan. "We know you can give the power of protection to whomever you want, whenever you want. We know it's basically bulletproof."

I had the feeling then that she'd rushed through more tests she wasn't telling us involving guns and knives and arsenic, but I didn't ask, and she didn't elaborate.

Instead she pulled what looked like a complicated walkie-talkie out of her bag and turned it on. The sound of static filled the loft as she set it on the table between us, its oblong screen glowing orange.

"We're obligated to do some good," said Oh. "We have to."

"What is that thing?" I asked. Something about the object on the table made me nervous.

"It's a police scanner. I got it at Larry's."

"Who's Larry?" I said, setting aside for a second that we were probably doing something illegal.

"Larry's Telecom in West Salem. It's no big deal," said Oh. "Lots of people have them. It's so you can listen in on what's going on in the underbelly of our fine city. Cool, huh?"

The radio sparked to life with the sound of two voices. One sounded like a dispatcher, the other a police officer. They were talking about a domestic disturbance at a house on Franklin Street.

"Oh, you can't be serious about this," I said.

"Of course I'm serious! How could I not be? You've got an incredible gift and you have to share it. What's not to be serious about?"

"You want me to break up domestic disputes? In case it's not obvious, I don't have any ninja skills."

Oh didn't find my joke humorous. "You're always making light of things, Jacob. Who knows how long this is going to last or how many people you could save? Last night I listened to that thing in bed for hours. It was mostly accidents or heart attacks, not crimes, but there was plenty of mayhem going on while you slept."

"This is actually starting to sound pretty cool," said Milo.

129

"You're both out of your minds!" I yelled. "Forget it, forget the whole thing. And while you're at it, forget I ever found out about the diamond or the argyle or whatever you want to call it. I'm not doing this anymore."

I was so frustrated I wanted to throw myself out of the loft, and being unkillable, I went ahead and did it. I got out of my chair and dove right off the edge toward the floor. It would have been better if I hadn't hit the table full of books and broken one of the legs off, but either way, it was just what the doctor ordered.

"You okay down there?" asked Oh.

"Stop breaking stuff, man!" said Milo. "You're killing me!"

They both came down the ladder and found me sitting cross-legged on the floor, surrounded by books that had fallen off the small table. Oh put her hand on my back and made little circles, which was electrifying right down to my toes.

"Lemme fix this table," said Milo. He was monkeying around behind us trying to fit the busted leg back into its slot.

"I know it's scary and weird," Oh said quietly, "but we can't do nothing, Jacob. We can't."

"Why not?"

I was loaded with confusion, but Oh's amazing hand on my back was helping me feel better.

"Do you want to know why we moved here?" she asked. It felt like Oh was switching tactics, searching for a way to convince me of her point of view.

I looked in her eyes, searching for what kind of answer she might give to her own question.

"My mom's boyfriend went a little haywire after he lost his job. They fought all the time."

"Dude, that sucks," said Milo.

"Sorry," I added, not knowing what else to say. It wasn't new territory for me.

"He never touched us, but my mom had a bad feeling after a while. Too much yelling and a couple of things got thrown across the room. It wasn't like her to put up with that kind of thing for very long. We packed up in the middle of the night while he was passed out in front of the TV," said Oh.

She paused, took her hand off my back, and ran it across the words I'd written on her cast. "I never felt safe at home. But I do now."

I could imagine myself stepping into Oh's old house to the sound of yelling. I could see the bloodshot eyes of a drunk man in jeans and a dirty white T-shirt. He'd be good-looking in all the wrong ways, trying to look younger than he really was. He'd see me enter the front door and yell some profanity at me about what was I doing in his house and who did I think I was. He would push me out the door, thinking I was a kid, but I would resist. He'd punch me, which would hurt his hand but not my face. He'd get uncontrollably angry and grab an empty beer bottle by its neck, raising it to clobber me...

"This is getting super heavy," said Milo, backpedaling

toward the wall where he pretended to peruse the mystery books.

"How can we know what we have and do nothing?" Oh asked in a guarded whisper. "Maybe you can, but I can't."

I imagined the same scene at Oh's old house with her in it instead of me, vulnerable, in the kind of trouble no teenager deserved.

It made me feel like I would do anything for her.

"All right," I said, "we take it slow, nothing too crazy. If we're lucky Ethan will calm down and Holy Cross will stay open until we graduate. Who am I to stand in the way of saving a few lives along the way?"

It was decided that Oh would be in charge of the police scanner. Technically it was against the law to listen in and share information you heard with someone else, so we would need to be extremely careful.

I got up off the floor to stretch what should have been my broken back.

"Doesn't it feel strange, knowing you should be dead but finding that you're not? It's kind of, I don't know, invigorating, don't you think?"

Oh's question took me by surprise, because I really hadn't thought of it that way. I was beginning to take the long view of death. The *really* long view.

"Speaking of death, should we show her the Isengrim?" asked Milo. "I think she can be trusted."

Milo made a point of pronouncing it with an emphasis

on the "eye": the EYE-Zin-Grim. It was a superb name for an object of curiosity. I'd only ever seen the Isengrim a few times, and after talking to Mr. Coffin I had a whole new set of feelings about it.

"What's the Isengrim?" asked Oh.

Milo was up out of his chair, heading down the ladder.

"You have to see it to believe it. Come on."

◆　◆　◆

Milo went behind the counter and flopped into his mom's ancient La-Z-Boy. Below the cash register, there was a small safe with one of those dialing locks on the front. Milo's parents were supposed to be the only ones who knew the combination, but Milo had found it long before I met him, written on the underside of the money tray in the cash register. He spun the dial from memory, and I knew he'd gotten what he was searching for when I heard the sound of jangling keys.

"Your parents have a lot of things locked up," said Oh, seeing the twenty or more keys on a silver janitor's ring in Milo's hand.

"It's all my dad's doing. He's like a magnet when it comes to finding weird old stuff."

"This isn't the part where we find the axes and the hammers, is it?" asked Oh.

Milo and I crossed the store and stood under the loft, where one of the bookshelves was held by monstrous metal hinges. They were painted black and hard to see in the soft light. Milo dropped the ring of keys in my hand and pulled on the side of the shelf, throwing all of his weight toward me. It swung open agonizingly slowly, groaning on hinges that seemed barely able to hold the weight of so many books. A hidden door was revealed behind the shelf.

"This is *so Munsters*," said Oh, watching Milo unlock and pry open the door. "You don't really expect me to go down there?"

Milo smiled and started down into the darkness, the stairs creaking under his small frame.

Oh grabbed my hand like we were about to enter a haunted house on Halloween. She didn't look at me, only down the stairs as the cold, earthy air drifted into our faces.

"Is there a light down there?"

The tinny sound of a chain being pulled against a single bulb echoed up the stairs and the dimmest light crept up toward us.

"Depends on what you mean by light," I said.

"If you guys are setting me up to scare me—"

"I'd never do that."

I guided her down the stairs, holding her hand tight as we passed under low beams. I could feel her tense as I tugged her deeper into the basement.

"Trust me," I said, gazing back up at her silhouette. "I haven't gotten you killed yet, have I?"

"Come on, you guys, it's getting lonely down here," said Milo.

It was an old basement of cinder block and crumbling masonry. Two of the walls were lined with racks full of items a person might expect to find in a dungeon repair shop. There were shackles, ball and chains, iron bars, and maces. What looked like a portable guillotine on wheels sat in one corner, along with a box shot through with swords.

Oh looked around the space in a state of nervous curiosity, her eyes scanning a concrete wall filled with posters and images. There was a yellowed and curled image of a man releasing a bird from a box, another of a man spouting a stream of water over a crackling fire, and a collection of posters for fantastic events at theaters around the world.

"Is that what I think it is?"

Her eyes had settled on the overpowering object in the middle of the room. All the oddities in the basement faded into oblivion in the imposing presence of the Isengrim.

"If you think it's an electrocution device, you got it right," said Milo. "It's my dad's prized possession."

"How did you turn out normal?" asked Oh, walking around the oblong, waist-high table. Each side was home to many wooden drawers, but the top was a dead giveaway.

"Why on earth would anyone build something like this?"

The top of the table was a sheet of brushed iron or metal. There were clasps for ankles and hands, levers, and wires running along the floor and disappearing under a shelf of junk.

"Okay, so here's the deal," said Milo, the tour guide in him revving up to full speed. "You won't believe this—hell,

I didn't even believe it—but according to my dad, this thing was Houdini's idea, some sort of escape trick he was working on right before he died. The idea was he'd lie down and get all shackled to the table, right? Then they'd wire him all up like Frankenstein's monster and turn this dial to set the clock for three minutes. Once the dial was set, there was no way to turn it off. So if Houdini didn't escape in three minutes, well, he was toast. Literally."

Milo started cycling through the keys and inserted one into the keyhole of one of the many drawers on the side of the Isengrim.

"See for yourself."

Milo had taken out a stack of old papers and laid them out on the metal top of the Isengrim. We all leaned over to look, casting head-shaped shadows from the bulb over our heads. The diagrams were very detailed, showing not only the making of the Isengrim, but the theatrics of the trick itself. The drawings included everything from a test subject to the final escape.

"*Eew,*" said Oh.

"I know, it's gross, isn't it?" I said. "First they had to show everyone that it actually worked. Who knew feathers would fly everywhere when you electrocute a chicken?"

"I think that was part of the problem with the Isengrim," Milo said, shaking his head. "If he doesn't make it, everyone has to watch him fry in the theater."

"Sounds like something some folks would pay a lot of money to see, actually," Oh commented.

Milo put the papers back and shut the drawer, locking it with a key.

"What's in the other drawers?" Oh asked.

"Other stuff my dad collects. Tricks, weapons, cards, old manuscripts, stuff like that."

After talking to Mr. Coffin, I saw the Isengrim and everything else in the basement in a different light. I wondered if Mr. Fielding hired Mr. Coffin to find some or all of this stuff. Why he wouldn't keep it himself, though, was a complete mystery to me.

"My dad would kill me if he knew we were down here," said Milo. "Can you imagine what it would be worth if it were the real deal?"

Oh glanced at Milo, trying to understand. "You're telling me he *built* the Isengrim down here? I thought he found it on eBay or something," said Oh.

"He used a set of plans. That much I know is true."

Oh ran her hand along the sleek metal surface, intrigued. "Does it work?" she asked hesitantly.

"Hell, no! But here's the crazy thing," said Milo, looking at the table and the wires leading away from it. "It *could* work, know what I mean?"

We'd tinkered with the Isengrim before — despite knowing what Mr. Coffin would do if he caught us — and we had a pretty good idea what wires would have to go where in order to juice the thing.

"My dad followed the plans to a certain point, then stopped. But it's close. Creepy, huh?"

Oh seemed to have lost her voice, so Milo kept going.

"You'd be surprised how much of this kind of thing goes on. There's like a whole black market for artifacts and lost notebooks and manuscripts. Someone offered him fifty thousand for this thing, but he wouldn't take it."

"I think Mr. Fielding might have known about it," I blurted out, not really thinking about what I was saying. "It's possible he even paid your dad to find or build it."

"I wouldn't be surprised," Milo agreed. "He used to come around a lot, before you, I mean. He and my dad were always talking."

I nodded, trying to piece things together.

"What else are you two not telling me?" asked Oh.

"I didn't think it mattered before, but it kind of adds up, when you think about it," I said. "If Mr. Fielding had this power before I did, and thought he could never die...well, then he'd probably have been fascinated with death."

Oh pulled out her notebook and began scribbling and mumbling. "You guys are full of surprises...."

When she was finished, she ran her hands along the Isengrim like she was thinking about making an offer to buy it.

"Let's get out of here," I said. "It's getting late."

Milo pulled the chain on the light, and Oh fumbled for my hand. *Thanks, Milo, I owe you one.* The only light that remained flooded in softly from the store above, showing us the way out. Milo started up the stairs as Oh put her arms around my neck and pulled me into a hug. Her cast lay stiff and heavy on my shoulder.

I felt her soft breath on my neck and pulled her closer.

"Get up here, you guys!" Milo yelled down the stairs.

Oh pulled away and we locked eyes on each other.

"Foiled again," I said.

NINE
DAYS TO
MIDNIGHT

FRIDAY, OCTOBER 12TH

On Friday at two AM, all hell broke loose.

I woke to the sound of my phone vibrating. I'm not in the habit of sleeping with my phone, but Oh insisted. She wanted to make sure I could respond if something really bad came up on the police scanner.

I stared into the blue light of my cell phone.

Fire. Get up!

I bolted out of bed and sat on the windowsill, where the cold window touched my bare shoulder blade. I started typing out an answer, but couldn't finish before the phone went off in my hand, a call coming in from Oh.

"Give it to me!" she yelled into the phone.

"Slow down, Oh—what's going on?"

"You're going to be too late! Just send it! Now!"

My head was receiving confusing signals. She needed the power, something was wrong, I wanted to trust her...

But I didn't want to give up what I had.

"Please, Oh—just tell me where you are. You're scaring me. What's the situation? Is everyone safe?"

"No, everyone's not safe! I'm standing in front of my building and it's on *fire*. Give it to me!"

"I can be there in ten minutes if I run. I'm fast—"

"Jacob—*God*—ten minutes and it'll be too late. I'm going in. Do whatever you want."

"Is the fire department there?" I asked, pulling on a pair of jeans.

No answer. Oh had hung up.

"Dammit, Oh!" I yelled. This turned out to be a terrible idea in a quiet house full of retired priests. There was a knock at my door as I pulled on a sweatshirt and a pair of shoes, locked my mind on Oh's face, and said the words.

You are indestructible.

Father Tim opened the door looking sleepy-eyed and worried.

"What's going on? Bad dream?" he asked.

"Come on," I said urgently, and brushed past him. "I need a ride to Oh's building! Please?"

Father Tim knew me well enough to know something bad was going down. As we walked along the hallway, a door opened and one of the old guys peered out, wondering what all the fuss was about.

"Back to bed, George—everything's fine," I heard Father Tim say.

We raced to the parking lot, and I tried to call Oh back, but got nothing but her flirty voice mail greeting.

"You got Oh—leave a message or don't—I'm good either way."

"Jacob, what's this all about?"

Father Tim was digging in his robe pockets, searching for a pack of Salems as we backed out of the parking lot.

"Oh's apartment complex is on fire. She just called me."

Father Tim lit a smoke and hit the gas harder than I thought was prudent for a priest with something way shy of 20/20 vision. The cigarette dangled from his lips, and I felt the first overpowering sting of secondhand smoke in my nose.

"Did she call you? Is she in the building?"

"I'm not sure where she is," I said, rolling down my window and letting the cold misty air swirl into the car.

I kept calling for ten blocks until we arrived in front of the apartment complex and saw flames licking up the side of one of the buildings, black smoke rolling on white siding.

My phone buzzed with a text message. Milo. Why in the world was he texting me at two AM?

In trouble. send diamond

"You've *got* to be kidding me," I said.

"What? What's wrong?" asked Father Tim as he slammed

on the brakes in the parking lot and we both got out. Fire trucks and cop cars lined the street.

My thumbs flew over the keypad. *Can't. call me!*

The air was already heavy with rain, and the fire made it feel thick at the back of my throat. There were four free-standing buildings in all with the parking lot in the middle. Oh's building hadn't caught fire, but the one right next to it was in serious trouble. Gawkers were standing everywhere, but I didn't see Oh.

"Is anyone in there?" I yelled.

"Just stay back!" yelled a police officer. "They've got it under control."

"My cat's in there," a lady in a ratty coat mumbled.

"Screw your cat, lady!" said an overweight older man in a T-shirt, boxer shorts, and black socks.

"Hey! My cat matters to *me*, okay?" the woman barked back, her voice shaking.

Father Tim, used to taking some level of control as a man of the cloth, stood between the two of them, speaking softly. "Are there any *people* inside?"

"My daughter is!" I whirled around and saw Oh's mom, a look of terror on her face.

"Ms. Henderson ain't been seen," said another man. "I told her not to take a room up there. She can barely make the stairs."

"How many are in there after them?" I asked.

"Don't know, three, maybe four firemen went in a few minutes ago," commented one of the onlookers.

My phone rang. Milo. I couldn't deal with this.

Meanwhile, the power wanted back in. I could feel it, burning my chest as if it was heating up. I knew Oh was in there because I could feel *it* was in there with her. But it was still all I could do not to say the words and get it back.

The phone stopped ringing. Whatever trouble Milo was in, he'd have to figure it out on his own.

The crowd erupted in shouts, and I glanced at the second floor where a hose was firing water into a window. Oh's head poked out from the flames, inexplicably untouched. She stared out into the night like a phantom, then disappeared as if she'd been pulled back inside.

As smoke billowed from the window, my phone buzzed three times with a text. I looked numbly at the screen.

> *E and B came after me. they're gone. it's 2 late. keep it. thanks a lot bro.*

No way. A two AM run on Milo's house? Insane. And besides, what could I have done? This was life or death — if I take the power from Oh, she's dead in there. And I was completely useless to help him without the power. No diamond, no protection.

The crowd lurched forward and right past the police officer as Oh emerged out of the smoke on the exterior stairs leading to the first floor.

"Oh my God," shrieked her mom, running past everyone until she was stopped by a fireman directly in front of the building. "Let me go!" She was wailing for Oh, punching and kicking the fireman who wouldn't let her get any closer. A police officer stepped in and wrapped his arms around Oh's mom, holding her still as she sobbed.

"It's okay, Ma! I'm fine! Calm down!" Oh shouted.

Two firemen approached her as she crept slowly down the outer stairwell, holding hands with an old woman who was holding a cat in one arm. The cat leaped free and ran into the brush beside the building as the firemen grabbed for Oh and the lady, pulling them out into the open parking lot. Three more firemen poured out of the building, one of them signaling that the place was now empty.

"Oh!" I yelled, breaking through the crowd and running past her mom. No one tried to stop me. Oh's shirt was scorched, her bra exposed. I pulled off my sweatshirt and approached her bare-chested and shivering.

"You're okay," I said.

I put the open circle of my sweatshirt over Oh's head as her mom came running, finally free to embrace her daughter. Her mom sobbed and kept saying "Are you okay?" and "Why did you do that?" over and over again. Looking over her mom's shoulder, her face wet with tears, Oh mouthed two words:

Thank you.

I nodded with a light smile, pulling the power back into myself and feeling its force surge through my veins.

When I looked at Oh again, I was surprised to find her gaze had changed. There was a kind of simmering rage in those flaming eyes of hers, like I'd taken something precious that belonged to her.

I pointed gently to my chest and whispered, "I have it. Don't go in there again."

She nodded and the angry look vanished as she clung closer to her mom. They'd just survived another catastrophe.

I felt the warmth of clothing on my back and shivered, awakened to the fact that I'd been standing in the drizzling rain without a shirt on. Father Tim had taken off his frizzy blue robe and draped it over my shoulders.

"Keep your hands off the smokes," he said as I plunged my hands into the soft pockets and felt the pack and the lighter.

I drifted back from the crowd, taking in the whole nightmarish scene as I watched thick smoke swirl grotesquely into a black sky.

We did it. We saved these people.

But with the smoke, the screaming, the spectacle, and Oh's momentary fury—somehow it all felt...wrong.

My phone rang, jarring me out of the stupor. "Milo? That you?"

"Yeah it's me. Where the hell were you?"

His voice didn't sound right, like he had a mouth full of peanuts.

"Oh got into some trouble. There was a fire, but she's okay. I had to let her have it."

Milo forgave me for leaving him in the lurch—he's cool like that—but didn't let me off without a guilt trip.

"They were pissed, man."

"What happened?"

"Tried to paint HOMO on my car door. Too bad for me I'm a light sleeper, and the sound of those shaking cans woke me up. By the time my dad woke up, me and Ethan were screaming at each other in the driveway."

"What'd they do?"

"We wrestled around on the lawn but he got in a shot. Right in the mouth. Hurts like a mother."

"It's okay—maybe it'll calm him down."

"Doubt that," said Milo. I heard him spit into a cup on the other end.

"I got a hold of that can when my dad came out and broke things up. Sprayed the crap out of that fancy sports car of his."

What a stupid ass move that had been. Couldn't Milo just take a punch and let it go?

"You shouldn't have messed with Ethan's car. He's crazy about that thing."

"He messes with my car, I mess with his. Simple as that."

"You need to learn to control your temper, man. I won't always be here to protect you."

"So I just learned."

"This thing is escalating. Just let him get the upper hand and forget about it."

"Screw that. We've got something he can't even begin to deal with. Let him run me over with his car. It ain't gonna matter."

"Dammit, Milo!" It was 2:30 in the morning. ⟍
friend and my new girlfriend were stirring a horne
into a frenzy. They just didn't get it. "You better h
doesn't drive over your ass when you can't find n
help."

"Jacob Fielding, cussing like a sailor. Glad to have
back."

"I gotta go. Oh's coming over."

"Tell her she's awesome. Flamegirl and all that. See y⟨
tomorrow."

The crowd was starting to thin into groups of four o
five on the sidewalk. Some people were heading back inside
Oh's building as the flames came under control. One guy
had brought out a lawn chair in which he sat and happily
drank a can of beer.

"They want to ask me some questions, and my mom
wants me back inside. I just wanted to explain—I mean, I
know I caught you off guard."

She ran a finger under her eye, catching a last tear.

"We saved someone tonight."

I looked past Oh and saw the person she'd gone in after
being loaded into an ambulance. The lady had an oxygen mask over her face and her chest was heaving as she
coughed the soot out of her lungs.

I was dying to grab Oh by the hand, pull her running
down the street to a quiet place where we could whisper,
our foreheads touching in the dripping rain.

"How'd it start?" asked Father Tim, looking at Oh as if

e had a special way of drifting
unnoticed. "Let me guess, one

te between two fingers, raising his

it got going," said Oh. "But a lot of
place. It wouldn't surprise me. I think
ond floor."

pt looking at Oh. He was avoiding the
veryone else was—*how did you get in and
thout being injured?*—but he wasn't saying
ade me wonder how much he knew, what Mr.
ght have told him, and if Father Tim had seen
like this happen before.

asy voice from behind Oh broke the moment.

ink you." The cat lady.

e was under a bed, not very happy to come out," Oh
ained.

"It's a she," said the lady.

"She's got sharp claws," said Oh, smiling at the woman. A police officer, jotting in a wet notebook, waved Oh over and she pulled away, our moist fingers slipping past each other. Her mom put an arm on her shoulder, and the two of them walked back to their own apartment with the officer.

Oh glanced back at me, and I got one more fleeting look at her face before she turned and walked away. It had changed again, revealing something she was struggling to hide. If I didn't know better, I would have said there was a craving in her expression, as if I had something she wanted more than anything in the world.

"Crazy night," said Father Tim, watching Oh curiously. He turned to me with an eyebrow raised, but when I looked away he seemed to let it go, focusing on the priestly work that would keep him out of bed for at least a few more hours.

"I know a lot of these people," he said. "Better stay awhile, make the rounds. You want to wait in the car where it's warm?" He held the keys out to me, but I didn't feel like sitting in the car waiting for the night to pass.

"You mind if I keep this and walk?" I lifted the pockets of the heavy robe, feeling guilty for having asked.

"It's a pretty good hoof from here. You sure?"

"I'm sure."

Father Tim ran a hand over his salty red beard. "I've got some provisions in the car. Come on."

Leave it to a priest in dreary Oregon to always come prepared, regardless of the time. We walked to the car and Father Tim clicked open the hatchback. A couple of tennis racquets, a metal basket of tennis balls, two umbrellas, a winter coat, at least two wadded-up sweatshirts that hadn't been washed in ages.

"Take this," he said, handing me an umbrella and pulling out one of the old tops. "And this."

I peeled off the robe and put on a sweatshirt that smelled mildly of church incense. By the time I had the robe back on, there were three people standing nearby, waiting to talk to the local priest.

"Don't wake the old guys," said Father Tim as he pulled on his coat. "They get cranky." He held out his hand and I dug in the pocket of the robe, fishing out the Salems and a plastic lighter.

"Good lighter?" I asked, thinking of the Zippo I'd gotten from Mr. Fielding.

"I'm marking time, waiting till you give me the good one."

"You'll be waiting a while."

Father Tim laughed softly, turning to talk to the people waiting.

"You must have known him a lot better than he ever let on," I added, probing for information.

"I'm a safe bet. He could tell me a lot and knew I wouldn't blab."

"That must be hard, keeping secrets all the time."

He eyed me cautiously. "Comes with the job. You get used to it."

"Did he ever tell you how old he was? For some reason he never told me, even though I asked him more than once."

Father Tim's eyes narrowed as he looked up into the drizzle, wiped the water from his brow.

"He never told me, but if I had to guess, I'd say he looked young for his age."

He shut the trunk of his car, and we both looked back at the group of people hovering close by. "I better get into the mix here, Jacob. Get back home and settle in. I have a feeling this is going to take a while."

I took a last look at the sizzling apartment building and

started for the church house. There was something sorrowful but sweet about the stillness. As the smell of smoke thinned and disappeared, I thought about Oh, Milo, Father Tim, and Mr. Fielding. Those looks from Oh, the fire, Ethan's temper—the whole crazy mess we'd gotten tangled up in was starting to feel like we were in way over our heads. The trust between me and Oh and Milo felt fragile, like everything could break apart at any moment.

If there was even a chance of discovering something that might help us, could I really wait another week to go searching for what Mr. Coffin had found? I'd been putting off going to the coast at all cost, because things happened on that last drive with Mr. Fielding that terrified me. Stuff I didn't want to relive any sooner than I had to.

◆ ◆ ◆

The next morning, Father Tim caught me at the front door of the church house and asked me about his robe. I'd left it in a wet pile on my floor, where it was bound to smell musty by the time he got back, he pointed out. Sighing, I slipped back upstairs, taking care to avoid the kitchen scene. I'd had enough of Father Frank, Father David, and Father Joe standing around the coffee pot, scratching everything, blowing their noses and checking out the damage on their grubby handkerchiefs, and asking a string of pointless questions. Give them an inch and they'd gobble up twenty minutes without batting an eye.

On my way back out, I squeezed past Father Tim and smelled the mossy air outside. "Did they figure out how the fire started?" I asked, stepping out onto the weed-infested cracks of the front steps.

"I think the cat was involved," answered Father Tim, his funny bone still active even if he looked like the walking dead. He patted me on the shoulder and added, "Pretty old wiring in that place. It's amazing nothing happened sooner. Count our blessings no one got hurt."

"Yeah."

He pulled off his glasses and wiped them on a tiny rag he kept in the pocket of his black pants.

"Amazing how Oh came out. No coughing, no burns, nothing. You could do worse than date a girl like that. She's hardy."

He looked at me, and if I didn't know better, I'd have guessed he was looking for a reaction of some kind.

"I'm not exactly sure how to take that," I said. "You mean hardy like a Norwegian farmwife?"

"No, I mean she's got vitality."

He said it like he was really happy I'd found someone to take my mind off everything that had happened.

"Plus she's hot," I said.

"You got me there."

I started to walk away, but he wasn't done talking yet.

"Can we talk later, maybe after school?"

"Uh, yeah, sure—let me check with Milo, see what's up. Maybe you should take a nap between now and then."

"You read my mind."

I just hoped that Father Tim couldn't read mine.

◆ ◆ ◆

Friday morning at school Oh seemed genuinely happy, one might even say bouncy. She was a hero (the paper would later confirm), and, better still, she was spending the weekend with her dad in Eugene to see the Oregon Ducks play USC.

Every chance I had between classes I'd scan the circular hall, find her, and pull her into a private moment of whispering.

You can't run into burning buildings with a bunch of people standing around. People will talk.

Father Tim is getting too curious. Let's make sure we chill out for a few days, okay?

You sure you have to go away this weekend?

Twenty minutes after lunch, sitting in Miss Pines's class talking about *The Once and Future King*, my phone vibrated to life. Miss Pines wasn't as diligent about cell phones, especially when she was lecturing, so I pulled it out of my pocket and peeked down to have a look.

Something huge. can you get out of class?

I used one thumb to tap out the briefest of messages.

Meet park lot

I waited a few seconds, listening to Miss Pines ramble on about T. H. White and Thomas Malory and blah blah blah...

Now, not later. right now.

I raised my hand, asked to use the bathroom, and Miss Pines asked if I couldn't just hold it for five more minutes, and she'd be done with the lecturing part of the class.

"I don't think I can wait, Miss Pines."

She rolled her eyes while the rest of the class laughed quietly.

"Go on," she said, motioning for the door and acting as though she'd probably just wait until I got back to continue what she was saying. "I'm timing you."

"Yes, ma'am. I'll be quick."

Down the hall, past the bathrooms, turned to the right, and hit the bar on the door leading out to the lot. Oh was nowhere in sight. I started to head back, but my phone buzzed.

I can't get out! look at this face. her name is Lisa Moss. give it to her.

What the...? Oh had picture-mailed me a photo of a girl smiling. It looked as if it had been cropped out of a bigger picture, maybe one in which she was posing with her family. Lisa Moss looked about my age.

We'd never tested this before—a picture and a name, someone I'd never met. Where was she? Who was she? Why was I being asked to do this? It felt like I was a horse and Oh held the reins.

There's no way I'm doing this.

My phone buzzed again.

You're hesitating. i know you. just do it. please.

I tell her to take it easy and this is what I get. She's out

158

looking for places where this thing can be of some use in the world when she knows she should be laying low.

Just do it. Please. I could hear the sound of her voice in my head, feel myself wanting to please her more than ever.

I went back to the picture and stared. Who is this girl? A confident, athletic-looking teenager with curly black hair.

Oh, what the hell.

I took a deep breath, thought about what it was going to feel like to let it go again, and said the words out loud.

"You are indestructible."

"Don't I wish."

I spun around and saw Miss Pines, arms folded, staring at me.

"Oh crap."

"Yeah, oh crap. You take me for a fool, Jacob?"

"No—not at all Miss Pines. It's just—"

"Just what? Spit it out."

But I had nothing. I felt the power leaving my body. My head turned dizzy for a brief second, like I was falling, and I touched the brick wall of the school to steady myself.

"You taking drugs? Is that what this is?"

"No, honestly Miss Pines—I just needed some air. I wasn't feeling very good."

"Well, why didn't you say so? Come on, I'll take you to the office, and you can lie down, get some water."

"It's okay, I'm feeling better. The fresh air helped."

She gave me that sideways look, her expression split between concern and suspicion.

"You sure there's nothing wrong? You can tell me, it's okay."

I nodded, said I was fine, and we started back to the classroom.

"Do me a favor, will you?" she asked. "When you leave my class, go where you say you're going, okay? You'll get us both in a lot of trouble if you keep wandering off like that."

"Got it, no problem."

"I'm keeping you after class for an hour, for lying to me."

"But Miss Pines, I won't—"

She put up a hand, smiling lightly as we approached the door.

"No consequences, no change in behavior. That's the way it is with me, you should know that by now."

It was a worse punishment than she knew. Oh was leaving on a bus to her dad's right after school. I was planning to drive with her and Milo to the station downtown. We both bugged her about how slumdog a bus ride was, but she loved it. Her dad had offered to come get her, but an hour and a half of watching farms roll by was exactly what she wanted.

"Can I make this up to you some other way?" I pleaded. "Or maybe, I don't know, next week?" I asked as she opened the door and I heard people grab-assing inside.

"Look what you did to my class," said Miss Pines. "I've lost my momentum." Returning to an unruly class had put her in a rare, sour mood, and she wasn't budging. "How much T. H. White you all wanna read this weekend?" she barked at the class. *The Once and Future King*, while a decent book, was about a million pages. She could assign enough to keep us shackled to the book all weekend if she really wanted to.

I slumped down in my seat, the heat of a whole room of eyeballs boring down on me for starting trouble on a Friday afternoon.

My phone buzzed three times, but there was no way I was taking the chance. If I got caught checking my phone, it was over. I'd be reading T. H. White until my fillings fell out. It buzzed again. And again.

"Give it," said Miss Pines, holding out her hand from the front of the class. Everyone shuffled nervously in their seats, but the slight vibrating sound had come from only one phone and everyone knew whose it was.

"Jacob Fielding," Miss Pines said evenly, frighteningly. Oh man, I had rarely heard her use that kind of tone in front of a class. She was pissed. "Give me that phone."

I didn't know what to do. She'd check the texts. That's what teachers did. She'd check the pictures. They did that, too. There was a trail of bizarre information that would blow everything wide open. I felt like I was perilously close to working at the CIA protecting the president or walking into a bunker full of terrorists in Afghanistan.

My phone began to buzz again. I slid the battery off the back and handed the phone to Miss Pines as politely as I could.

"I'm really sorry about this," I said.

"You don't know the half of it."

Miss Pines jerked the phone out of my outstretched hand and returned to her desk. She could see I'd taken off the battery, but I got the feeling she didn't want to fight it out in front of the class.

Now that the phone was gone, I was dying of curiosity. What was this all about? When could I get the power back? It was scratching harder than before, more like it was biting my skin to get back inside. It was incredibly hard to concentrate.

Twenty-five long minutes later, the class filed out. Miss Pines waited until everyone else was almost gone, and then she came up to my desk and looked down at me. She did not look happy to be stuck with me for another hour.

"Stay put, big man. I'll be back." She followed the students out, carrying my battery-less phone in one hand and a copy of *The Once and Future King* in the other.

I had no way of telling Oh what was going on, no way of seeing her off to the bus station where I would have almost certainly enjoyed our first good-bye kiss.

My head hurt in the strangest way, like a brain freeze after drinking a Slurpee too fast. I closed my eyes and rubbed my temples, which is why I heard them coming in before I saw them. I expected to see Miss Pines gliding through the door with an afternoon cup of coffee retrieved from the teachers' lounge, but when I opened my eyes again I saw Oh and Milo standing over me.

"If she catches you guys in here, I'm beyond busted."

"You and me both," said Milo, his lip still fat from the night before.

"Tell me you did it," said Oh. A day was coming when I would disappoint her, fail some request she'd made of me. I was happy that day hadn't come yet.

"Whoever Lisa is, she's indestructible. At least she is if it works. I don't know."

But I did know. If the power *wanted* back inside me this badly, Lisa had to have it.

"Put your hand out on the desk," said Oh. "I've got something for you."

I tentatively moved my hand out, palm up, and she took out a pencil.

"I don't think that's necessary," I said. "I'm telling you she's got it."

"Only one way to be sure," said Oh. She put the tip of the pencil against my skin and held it there, looked up into my eyes hopefully. Then she pushed, softly at first then harder, until the sharp tip of the pencil made me wince in pain.

"Awesome," said Oh. I expected her to smile brightly with those incredible eyes. But she didn't. First she looked euphoric, as if some drug had been pumped into her veins, but then, just as suddenly, the anger in her eyes returned, and she glared at me, digging the pencil a little deeper into my hand.

"Cool it, Oh! That hurts," I told her, annoyed. Did I just

not know her well enough to understand these flashy mood swings that couldn't be explained?

She yanked the pencil away, like she'd been caught doing something she shouldn't. Her smile returned, but it was covering up something else she was feeling.

"I wish I could do that, save someone like you do. It must be an incredible feeling."

I was about to tell her no, actually, it hurt like hell and it comes with a lot of emotional baggage, when Miss Pines stepped into the room.

"Out, both of you."

Oh swiftly pulled a folded piece of paper out of her notebook and dropped it in my lap. Her back was to Miss Pines, blocking her view as I hid the paper inside my desk and Milo started chatting up Miss Pines.

"You ever think about writing a ghost story, Miss Pines? Kids love that sort of thing. It'd be even better if you could do it in 3-D."

"Very funny, Mr. Coffin."

"No, I'm serious. It's never been done. All you gotta do is insert a set of 3-D glasses into the back of the book and put some freaky pictures in there that only show the ghost if you use the glasses. It's a bestseller waiting to happen."

Miss Pines seemed to momentarily contemplate how such a ridiculous idea might work, then shooed Oh and Milo out of her room. Oh looked back at me, smiling like she was really going to miss me and wished we could sneak in a better good-bye.

"Call it Cheese Zombies," Milo recommended from the hall as the door closed. "That'd be huge! I'm telling you—bestseller!"

The door clicked shut, and Miss Pines shook her head. "His head is in the clouds, just like yours."

"When do I get my phone back?" I asked, dying to text Oh and Milo as they went off into the world without me.

"Monday, unless you really make me mad, then it's going to be longer."

"Miss Pines! You can't do that—I *need* my phone this weekend!"

"Not my problem."

She sat down at her desk and flipped open her laptop. I pulled out my copy of *The Once and Future King* and had been reading the same sentence for three minutes when Miss Pines sighed heavily.

"Oh," said Miss Pines. "That's terrible." She shook her head. "Nothing but bad news," said Miss Pines. "It gets old."

"What is it?" I asked, already feeling the dreaded weight of responsibility to help before I even knew what she was talking about.

"A teenage girl went paragliding in Oceanside, and the wind shifted without any warning at all. She's out over the ocean. *Way* out."

I touched the folded piece of paper inside my desk. "Is she okay? What happened to her?"

Miss Pines clicked her mouse, refreshing a screen I

couldn't see. "She landed in the water, about two miles offshore."

I didn't care anymore about whether or not Miss Pines saw the piece of paper Oh had given me. I set my book down and unfolded the crisp white page. It was a print-out of the homepage for Yahoo. Oh had a library hour at the end of the day where students could get online and do research with one of four computers. The story had two pictures, one of a paraglider out over the crashing waves of the ocean, the other of Lisa Moss. It was the same picture Oh had sent me. On the margin of the paper Oh had written a note in pencil. *This is her. I'll miss you...Oh.*

My head felt like I'd contracted a permanent case of brain-freeze. The power wanted back in. I wanted this to be over.

For the remainder of the hour while I tried my best to read, Miss Pines gave me periodic updates on Lisa Moss, mostly because I wouldn't stop pestering her about it every ten minutes.

Lisa Moss, the updated story concluded, had experienced a miraculous event. She'd landed in the frigid Pacific Ocean and become hopelessly entangled in her parachute. The waves had pulled Lisa under before a boat could reach her, leaving only the bright red chute lying like a bloodstain on the surface of the water. But when they hauled the lines up and pulled Lisa Moss into the boat, she was alive. Cold, shivering, coughing up saltwater, but alive.

Miss Pines let me walk up to her desk and see the picture

of Lisa and her dad, hugging one another on the Oceanside dock.

We'd saved a life, me and Oh, and it felt exhilarating. I shook off the doubt I'd felt earlier. Oh was right: We were needed. But something didn't feel right.

I closed my eyes, took the power back, and felt the calming relief of its return.

Miss Pines sighed deeply, looking at her watch and then the door. "I guess that's good enough. You can go."

It was 4:10. Oh's bus was already gone.

"Can I please have my phone back?" I pleaded. "Oh's out of town and it's the only way I can reach her."

"Give me the battery and I'll give you the phone," she said.

There was no way I could risk letting go of the battery. Lisa's face was on it. My texts to Oh and hers to me were on it. I'd done a lousy job of covering my tracks.

"See you Monday," I said, hoisting my backpack onto my shoulder and walking to the door.

"Stay out of trouble, Jacob."

This was one weekend where I intended to do just that.

EIGHT
DAYS TO
MIDNIGHT

9:00 AM
SATURDAY, OCTOBER 13TH

I shuffled down the church house hall on Saturday morning and realized that having Oh gone for the weekend was, in some ways, a welcome relief. There would be no drama today, as far as I could figure, and Sunday would begin with church, float poetically into an afternoon nap at the house, and languish into the evening with my nose in a book.

"Did you see the paper?" asked Father Tim as I passed by his small study lined with books and painted icons of saints. The Virgin Mary, Peter, John, Luke (my personal favorite, very concise), they all stared down from the walls at the back of Father Tim's head as he ignored them, staring instead at the news of the present day.

I looked inside where he was draped in his standard blue robe, drinking a cup of coffee and smoking a cigarette with the paper laid out on the desk. The fire had happened too late to make the morning paper the day before, but now it was front page news and so was Oh.

"Ophelia James, a student at Holy Cross Academy, went back into the burning building and returned with Miss Morgan at her side, who carried a cat."

"That's my girl," I said, stepping all the way inside the room.

"How's it going in that department?" asked Father Tim.

"Somehow I don't think you'd be the first person to ask."

"Don't be so sure. I wasn't always a priest, you know."

He looked out over his bifocals and sipped his coffee.

"Strong or weak?" I asked, eager to change the subject. Father Frank was known for making sinfully weak coffee....

"Frank's still asleep," said Father Tim, and I was off to the kitchen for toast and a big mug. When I returned I sat across from Father Tim and scanned the front page. The picture of Oh was breathtaking. She looked so vibrant, so alive. Nothing like a girl who'd just escaped from a flaming apartment should have looked.

"I still can't get over it," said Father Tim.

"I know," I mumbled, not sure what else I *could* say without sounding like I was trying to cover something up.

"You know, after you left she stayed around awhile, tried to be helpful. Never did cough, not even once."

"I talked to her today," I covered. "Turns out she wasn't

in there very long, and she never got into the really thick smoke."

Father Tim nodded, frowning. "Beautiful *and* lucky. Fabulous for you. Really, just fabulous."

Was he being serious or sarcastic? It was a fine line with a dry-witted priest.

"Can I ask you something?"

He took another sip of coffee, nodding over the rim of his cup.

"How long were you Mr. Fielding's priest?"

"Technically I wasn't his priest at all. We were friends. He didn't like going to church. Never could quite guilt him into it. But he always loved the school, and the history. I think he was a little afraid of being around a lot of people."

"Okay, then, how long were you his friend?"

"About twenty years, give or take. But he was gone for long stretches. He traveled a lot. In fact he traveled right up until he introduced you to me. Sometimes he was gone for a month, other times five years, and everything in between."

"Five *years*? You're kidding me." Where does someone go for five years? A person would have to live a whole different life.

"A lot of time in Europe and England and New York. Sometimes he came back with an accent, then lost it a few weeks later."

"I caught that," I said, thinking about how it was hard to tell where Mr. Fielding had come from, an international flavor creeping into a word or a phrase a few times a day.

"I know you weren't his priest, but did he ever confess to you?"

Father Tim didn't answer right away. I knew this was sacred ground, the confessions of the living and the deceased. If it was said in the box, it stayed in the box.

Finally, Father Tim said, "No. He never confessed anything to me. But then, sometimes a person will share mistakes more openly with a friend than with a priest. You understand what I mean?"

I felt a black dread bloom in my chest, the presence inside me clawing...not trying to get out, but moving like a cornered animal with its fangs bared in fear. The feeling made me catch my breath so violently I made a terrible sucking sound right in front of Father Tim.

"Be careful you don't choke on that toast. I'm a little rusty with the Heimlich."

He knew. Father Tim *knew*, I don't know, *something*, and he was playing with me.

"Is there anything you're not telling me?" I asked, ready to simply get things out in the open.

"Well, sure," said Father Tim. "There are ten thousand secret sins I can't tell you. Comes with the territory. But if you mean something about Mr. Fielding, then yes, there is something."

I braced myself, hoping he'd know, hoping he *wouldn't* know, feeling the black cloud in my chest pummeling my guts in search of a place to hide.

Father Tim opened one of the drawers in his desk and

pulled out a can of lighter fluid. For a split second, I have no idea why, I thought he might have plans to set me on fire and see for himself that I wouldn't die.

"Here, take this," he said, handing me the small tin can. "It was Mr. Fielding's, goes with the Zippo. When it stops lighting, you pull the center part out and pour some of this in there."

"That's it, that's all you wanted to tell me? That Mr. Fielding left a can of lighter fluid in here?"

Father Tim leaned on his elbows, staring right into my soul as only a priest can do.

"Mr. Fielding used to say he thought he might live forever. He was funny that way, always talking about some close call he'd had. Now I'm starting to see another pattern of close calls. One of my parishioners from the neighborhood saw Oh's accident on the street. They said it was pretty violent, the way it happened. And now Oh just about gets herself killed. I know she's a great girl, but danger seems to be drawn to her, Jacob. Or she's drawn to *it*. And remember, contrary to what Mr. Fielding used to say, no one lives forever."

I wanted to say, *wanna bet?* but I held my tongue. I couldn't tell if Father Tim knew anything about the power or not the way he danced around the subject so cleverly.

"Okay, I'll be careful. I'll take it slow."

"He was a good man, Jacob. Complicated, but good."

Father Tim excused himself and went to the kitchen for a fresh cup of coffee. I sat there, staring at Saint Luke, wondering if his life had been as difficult as mine was turning out to be. Whatever had taken up residence inside me had calmed down, as if it knew the threat from outside had vanished.

When Father Tim came back, I decided to ask him about one more thing.

"Did you hear about the girl at Oceanside?" I asked, biting into a piece of toast covered in peanut butter and honey.

"I did. It's a miracle she's alive. Things like that keep an old faith ticking."

"I never thought of it that way before."

"Wait until you're older. It's a long journey. Do you realize I'm almost twice as old as Christ was when he died? He's not the same to me as he was when I was thirty. It's like I'm old enough now he could be my kid, which is a freakish thought. Faith never stays put. It's always challenging, always questioning. That's what makes it real."

"You're a seriously deep thinker, you know that?"

He shrugged. "I'd love to hear more about this romance of yours."

"Sorry to disappoint you, but I don't want to talk about Oh. She's...*also* complicated, but I think I'm figuring her out."

"All right, then—but let me at least give you one piece of advice. Take it slow, like I said. And do something special, soon, a date she won't be able to forget. That's important."

"That's two pieces of advice. Can we move on?"

Father Tim waved me ahead.

"Did you mean what you said the other day, in religion class? About God saving everyone no matter what?"

"What do you think?"

I slugged down some coffee, stalling.

"I hope you were right."

Father Tim leaned in over his desk again with his fingers folded together.

"So do I."

I swerved the subject closer to where I wanted it to go.

"I was wondering about that girl, the one that landed in the ocean. She should have died, you know?"

"I know."

"Why didn't she? I mean, why her?"

"I guess it wasn't her time yet. When it is, she'll go."

"What if she was supposed to die but didn't? What then?"

Father Tim leaned back and looked out the window of his study. "Then God changed his mind. He's unpredictable."

No kidding, I thought. If Father Tim knew what I knew, his faith would be even more complicated. Why would God let a power like this fall into my inexperienced hands?

"God's into dangerous moves," I said, letting my train of thought slip out.

"I couldn't have said it better myself," said Father Tim.

"Dangerous moves. I like that. I might have to use it in a sermon."

"Consider it yours."

◆ ◆ ◆

I went back to the kitchen to use the house phone and see what Milo was up to, but I couldn't stop thinking about what Father Tim had said. God hadn't changed his mind, had he? We'd changed his mind for him, or so it seemed to me.

But then again...you *can't* change God's mind, can you?

That got me thinking: maybe those deaths that might have happened were...still out there somewhere. Death didn't just evaporate into thin air, did it? Maybe it was out there, getting bigger and darker, moving over our heads like a rain cloud about to burst.

Milo didn't answer, so I went back to my books, a dreary Saturday floating by. Setting the can of lighter fluid on my puny desk, I picked up *The Once and Future King*. What Father Tim had said about telling a friend my mistakes made me wonder. Did he know I was holding on to something about the day Mr. Fielding died? Could he see it in my face, the fact that I needed to tell someone? Probably.

I missed Oh, but that day it hit me just how much I missed Mr. Fielding. Maybe it was the loneliness. Being with Oh and Milo and having something totally outrageous to focus my attention on had been a reliable diversion. But a church house on a Saturday night is a stunningly still place. Mr. Fielding had been good to me. I hadn't let myself get very close to anyone like that before, and now that he was gone and I'd had a little time to really think about it, I felt the pain and understood the truth. Mr. Fielding was the closest thing to a dad I was ever going to have. I was too old for another chance. I was washed up in the son department. And it couldn't have happened at a worse time.

I inhaled deeply, thinking of the smell of pipe tobacco, and somewhere along the way I closed my eyes and slept like the dead.

SEVEN …
SIX …
FIVE …
FOUR DAYS
TO MIDNIGHT

8:20 AM
MONDAY, OCTOBER 15TH

I didn't see Oh again until Monday morning in the hallway at school. She looked tired but beautiful, with her hair pulled back in a ponytail. There were dark circles under her eyes, like she'd been out partying all weekend long, and it worried me.

"Hey, handsome, date any girls while I was gone?"

Her voice was as disarming as ever, so I played along.

"All seventeen of them."

"I'll have to think twice about leaving town again. I had no idea you were such a player."

"How was Eugene? You look worn out."

Oh shrugged and leaned against my arm heavily as we started walking toward our science class with Mr. D. "The football game was fun. Lots of college guys hitting on me, which drove my dad crazy."

"Glad I missed that. Did I mention the seventeen dates I had?"

She sighed, as if the fun had gone out of our banter.

"I took the police scanner with me."

Miss Pines had kept my phone all weekend, so there'd been no way to reach me.

"You should have given it a break, taken a couple of days off. It did wonders for me," I offered, feeling like she was letting the power take over her life and needed to back off. This seemed to anger her.

"Things happened, Jacob, things I could have changed if I'd had the power. I was useless down there."

She still wasn't looking at me as we walked at a snail's pace toward the main T in the hallway.

"Miss Pines had my phone."

"I know, Milo told me. Obviously he didn't relay my messages. I don't think he's as committed to this as you and I are."

"Or maybe he just wants to take it slow until we understand things better."

She stopped and looked at me, heated, confused, hurt.

"You left me out there without protection, Jacob. People were in trouble and I couldn't help. You have no idea how that feels."

We had come to the T, and she shook her head, backpedaling away from me.

"Come on, Oh. We can't save everyone."

Oh looked like she might start crying. I wanted to reassure her, but she wasn't interested in being comforted.

And then she turned away, wiping a tear that had bloomed under her eye but never fallen, and I knew I could never let her go. The thought of losing her made me so lonely inside I couldn't even let myself imagine it. She *needed* me to save, I could see that now. I needed to come partway toward her or risk losing everything.

I thought of her striking eyes, the part of her that had drawn me in from the beginning, how they were ringed in darkness like they hadn't been before. How many times had she tried to reach me? How long did she sit, hunched over the police scanner, searching for death in progress? No wonder she was tired and depressed.

An hour later Miss Pines gave me my phone along with a dire warning to keep it in my pocket or lose it for good. There was a part of me that almost wished I hadn't gotten it back. Life was way less complicated without it.

◆　◆　◆

We learned something new on Monday afternoon.

It started with Oh's police scanner: an old man having a massive heart attack. Oh was becoming a superior fact finder, and within five minutes she traced the street address to a real estate records file online, found the man's name— Lloyd Randall—entered it into multiple search engines, and found a picture of him. He worked for a local auto dealership. His picture was displayed as salesman of the month on their website.

I gave Lloyd the power, but the heart attack had already occurred.

Lloyd wasn't dead when I slipped him the diamond, but seven or eight minutes later, I felt the familiar scratching against my insides much more violently than ever before. It wasn't like the other times, when it merely *wanted* back in. This time it was more like it was a lion ripping me open, intent on crawling in whether I liked it or not.

I checked my watch, and Oh, ever the researcher, was able to find the time of death through some online wizardry I don't even want to know about. I got the power back at 9:13 PM. The time of death was 9:16 PM.

Had I killed Lloyd Randall by taking back the diamond?

"No," Oh said, but she looked bereft. It didn't help.

Milo jumped in. "No, she's right," he agreed. "The diamond *protects* a body from injury, doesn't *heal* an injury. In a case like this, or a stroke after it's underway, or a patient in a hospital…the injury has already occurred. So, the diamond can't, like, cure cancer. It all makes sense."

Milo's revelation was another tough fact I'd have to learn to live with: once someone was badly injured or really sick, it was too late for my kind of help.

♦ ♦ ♦

In the days that followed, we began to realize that it was going to be harder than we thought finding dangerous events in which the outcome wasn't already determined. Like we heard about a seven-car pileup on the I-5 in L.A. The trouble was, the accident had already happened and people were already dead, which made my power useless. The ones who hadn't died but were injured? I was also useless there, because the power couldn't change what had already happened.

It was a tricky business finding events that were in process where I could actually be of some help, and it drove Oh crazy whenever she found a horrible event online that had already occurred. Not being able to wrap her hands around death and rip it away was almost more than she could bear.

And then there was the depressing dilemma of wondering who, specifically, could be saved in a really big, catastrophic event in a place where I didn't know anyone. A hurricane is coming and it's probably going to kill some people. Who would I choose to protect? No clue. There's a war on, bodies piling up, which side would I choose? And then once I've chosen a side, which one person would I give the power to?

I wouldn't be able to handle that kind of decision unless someone flat-out told me who to save. And then what would I be? Someone else's tool for someone else's life-or-death judgment.

"Might as well pick me up and use me as a hammer."

That was how a really big fight got started between us early in the week.

"Fine by me," Oh responded. "I'll tell you who to save and when."

"Is that all you see me as, a tool?"

"Oh, you're a tool all right," Milo said, trying to make a joke that fell totally flat and got rewarded with Oh's smoldering gaze.

"Milo, I swear to God, if you don't stop with the stupid jokes, I'll kill you."

"Jacob, quick, give me the power. She's gone insane."

"Shut up!" Oh yelled a little overdramatically. Milo threw up his hands and walked out of the room. I expected Oh to go after him, but she seemed almost relieved to have him gone.

"He'll be back," she said, staring into a computer screen in search of an event in which I could be used. The dark circles from the weekend hadn't left, and I was starting to wonder how much sleep she was getting.

"Oh, listen, you have to stop taking this so seriously. You just about ripped Milo's head off."

Oh and I argued over this kind of thing for days. She was always arguing for more, more, more, and I was always asking her to slow things down. It became a sticking point for us, her mood growing darker at times. We were turning into that couple no one wants to be around, always fighting, and Milo chose to spend less time with us when we were together.

◆ ◆ ◆

On Tuesday Oh heard about a meth lab bust on the scanner at an old barn and knew there was a chance of an explosion. Apparently that stuff is very unstable. She'd gone to some trouble rounding up photos of most of the local police officers by the time I got to her, and when the call was radioed in, Sergeant Flowers was the first to arrive. There were other officers there as well, but protecting Flowers was the best I could do.

There was no explosion, so it didn't matter in the end—and this seemed to bother Oh a lot more than it should have. It was almost like she'd *wanted* an explosion to occur, and I had to remind her that no one had died, including Flowers, and that was a *good* thing.

Every time I slipped someone the diamond, it was harder to let it go. The clawing and scratching I felt increased the longer I left the power out, and sometimes I didn't think I could hold on as long as I needed to. This thing—whatever the hell it was—felt like a living, breathing monster of some kind. It would go out, save a life, then return angrier than ever, like it was pissed off at me for making it do its job. It was like a lion ripping at the door, totally enraged until it got in. I started to actually imagine it as a real lion like it had been somehow forced into my consciousness.

And there was something else, something really terrible that only I had to deal with. I had a full dose of good old Catholic guilt going full tilt 24-7 that Oh and Milo were immune to. They didn't have the power to save people; I did. And not helping people in danger every second of every day meant that people were dying needlessly. Every time I read something online about a catastrophe at sea or a hurricane blowing into a village, I felt I should have done something to save someone. By Wednesday I was avoiding the Internet altogether.

But that didn't stop Oh from finding more and more opportunities for heroism.

On Wednesday, it happened.

◆ ◆ ◆

Wednesday was the first time I killed a guy. Officially, that is. Well, I didn't really kill him, but I could have saved him, so in a sense I was responsible for what happened. I chose, he died. Not a good feeling.

The problem was timing. I had already given the power to one of two people who'd gone missing on Mount Hood and hadn't been seen or heard from for two days. The weather had turned, and they were trapped on the mountain with search teams out looking. It was the hardest save I'd performed because it took a long time, but I knew the climber was alive. I knew, because I had a terrible chill all day.

We watched the news online once school got out, and

it seemed like they were making progress. There was talk on the scanner about them being found and trying to move them off the mountain. Right in the middle of all that, a headline appeared on Yahoo! News and Milo elbowed me on the arm.

The story was front page, dead center, a picture of a woman crying. Her husband had been taken hostage at a bank after things went horribly wrong during a holdup. There were two gunmen, a ton of police officers, but only one bank employee held inside. I didn't know what to do. We all stared at the story, which included the picture of the hostage and a name: Mike Farmer. I had all I needed to save him, a name and a picture. They could shoot him in the head and it wouldn't matter.

But I was freezing cold, and I had the feeling that if I stopped protecting the person on Mount Hood he'd die before they could get him off the mountain.

"What should I do?" I asked, looking back and forth between Oh and Milo. If I saved one person, there was a real chance the other would die.

"Which one is more likely to get killed?" asked Oh. Her eyes darted to the screen, and she started clicking through different news sites looking for more details.

"You've been on that guy on the mountain all day," said Milo. "I think they have him anyway. He'll make it."

"For all we know, they've found him but can't get him down," I said.

"At least he's not alone. He's with a friend."

"I hate to be the one to tell you this, but I'm not keeping them both alive. Only the one that has kids, remember? We talked about this."

"I know, I know," said Milo, exasperated at how few details were surfacing online and through the police scanner.

"Maybe we need to think of this in a different way," said Oh.

"How?"

"Well, which one deserves to live more?"

Milo's mouth dropped open. "You're getting a God complex."

"No, I'm not," said Oh, her face narrowing as she bore down on Milo. "I'm trying to help Jacob make the right choice here. All I'm saying is one of them went up into the mountains voluntarily and basically screwed up. He didn't check the weather or whatever. He was thrill-seeking. Accidents happen. Plus he's probably already saved anyway. This guy at the bank is different. He just showed up for work and his day went to hell."

"Maybe he beat up his kids before he left the house," said Milo, turning sulky and irritable, like we were ganging up on him.

It could have been the seven hours of feeling cold. Maybe it was the unrelenting claws digging into my bones like a cancer. Or maybe I just wanted to side with Oh even when she was being sort of a punk about the whole thing. Regardless of why, the moment came when I relented.

"It's done," I said, feeling a wave of peace flow into my mind and body. I was warm, calm, happy.

"Done? How do you mean, done?" demanded Milo.

I got up and peeled off a coat, feeling sweat begin to trickle down the inside of my arm.

"The guy on the mountain is officially on his own."

Two hours later we discovered that Mike Farmer, the bank employee, had been let go unharmed. An hour after that, the news from Mount Hood wasn't so good. Both men were found dead, frozen to death in a snow cave of their own making.

All three of us were devastated. Not only had we let someone die, a parent no less, but the person we'd chosen to protect turned out not to need it after all. The whole weight of every decision, in the end, fell on me alone. I'd killed a guy, maybe two, trying to save someone who didn't even need saving. No matter how tightly Oh held on to me or how many times Milo said it wasn't my fault, the guilt was eating me alive.

The Mount Hood Bank Heist incident, as it came to be known between us, was not as traumatic as what happened on Friday.

NOON, THURSDAY, OCTOBER 18TH

It began on Thursday, when I was gobbling down cheese zombies at our usual table, passing the time with Milo, Phil, Nick, Oh, and a couple of other girls who had recently drifted into our hemisphere. I was ravenous all the time, downing two zombies and looking hungrily at Oh's, which sat untouched on a paper plate. She wasn't eating, wasn't sleeping, and I wasn't the only one who noticed her change in behavior. It was starting to become obvious to everyone that something was wrong.

"You're not going to believe where I'm going tomorrow morning," said Oh.

"The gynecologist," said Milo. Nick laughed until a gob of cheese left his mouth and landed on the floor.

"You're both idiots," said Taylor. Her friend June shook

her head in agreement, but seeing Nick spit cheese was hard to ignore. Even Phil was laughing, which was saying something with so many girls piled around the table.

"Try South Ridge," said Oh, avoiding my eyes.

"You're screwing with us," said Milo.

Oh shrugged her shoulders as everyone begged her to reconsider. I didn't say a word. I couldn't even begin to imagine Holy Cross without her.

"Look, you guys, I'm not *going* there. At least not yet. My mom is making me do it. I guess my dad has fallen behind on his payments a little bit. Too many football games."

"Me and Nick can go down there and beat the money out of his duck-loving weenie ass," said Milo, sending Nick into another fit of giggles.

"It's not his fault," said Oh, shaking her head and glancing at me for the first time to see my reaction. "And besides, this is nothing. I'll mow lawns if I have to. I'll get a paper route. Nothing's keeping me out of Holy Cross."

"Unless they shut 'er down," said Nick. "Father Tim's got another summit meeting in Seattle with the head honchos this weekend. If they don't fork over some dough pretty soon, this place is toast."

We all got quiet and awkward and ate our cheese zombies. It was one of those times I wished I could tell everyone what Father Tim and I knew about the money situation. But I couldn't. Better to let things play out naturally...at least until the end of the school year.

"You know," said Milo. "Your mom's probably playing it smart. Good to have a backup plan. Mind if I tag along?"

"Me, too," I said, the words catching in my throat. There was no school at Holy Cross on Friday—a church holiday we'd all been looking forward to—but South Ridge would be open, and there was no way I was letting Oh in there without me. College guys at a football game I can deal with, but not Ethan and Boone and the rest of the Holy Cross defectors at South Ridge. No way.

This was a silver lining, because Oh looked at me like she'd just gotten exactly what she'd asked for at Christmas. If not for the fact that I lived in a church house with a bunch of old farts, I think I could have taken her home and had my way with her, she was *that* happy I'd offered to go with her. I hadn't seen her look at me that way in days, and even in the darkness that seemed to be overpowering her at times, those bright eyes still delivered a knockout punch. The old Oh was still in there, and I felt we were going to be okay. She would adjust, we would learn.

We'd figure out how to bring the power under our control and get back to a normal life.

THREE
DAYS TO
MIDNIGHT

8:20 AM
FRIDAY, OCTOBER 19TH

Our timing was terrible when we arrived on campus in Milo's crapper of a car. Ethan and Boone, along with a whole bunch of other football players, were standing in front of the school acting like jockstraps. There were girls hanging on and nerds swinging wide in order to avoid the possibility of being called out. Ethan was laughing obnoxiously. Same old, same old.

Boone noticed us first and hit Ethan on the arm. Pretty soon the whole group of six or seven players were looking at us, most of them whistling at Oh.

"It's a mass exodus," said Boone as we came within earshot. He and Ethan both stepped into our path and one of the other players cat-called to Oh.

"Cost me six hundred bucks to fix my car," said Ethan. "Better crack open that piggy bank of yours."

"If you want to go another round, just say so," said Milo. This elicited a swooning cry of ooh's and oh's from the gathering crowd.

Ethan switched tactics, undoubtedly thinking about the whipping he'd taken from Milo in the Holy Cross parking lot.

He took a really good look at Oh up close. "You sick or something?" asked Ethan. "You don't look so hot."

I stepped closer to Ethan, a thin rage beginning to take hold.

"Calm down, bro," said Milo. "Let's just finish this and get out of here."

That line of reasoning went out the window as Oh passed by Ethan on her way inside. He took her by the arm and pulled her close, started talking about how he'd give her the grand tour, and I don't know what happened to me.

Maybe it was the stress, maybe all the pent-up guilt over the Mount Hood Bank Heist thing. Maybe it was the monstrous feeling that had taken up residence in my chest, making me feel darker and meaner all the time. I don't know what it was, but I let fly a punch that landed squarely on Ethan's forehead. I've never been in a fight, so yeah, my aim was a little off. Milo looked at me with surprised appreciation.

Ethan doubled over, then looked up at me like he was going to kill me. His forehead was already turning red.

"I'm really glad you guys came with me," Oh said, looking at me like I'd lost my mind.

The school bell went off, and it felt more like the sound of round one at an ultimate fighting match. The whole group of them surrounded us, and all I could imagine was Oh getting hurt in the crush. Milo could handle himself, but these were big guys.

I was right on the edge of windmilling the whole bunch of them when a teacher pushed the door to the school open and yelled for everyone to get inside. Ethan had his back to the teacher, along with four more wide bodies between them, and he took one good punch at my gut with all he had.

I should have buckled over. I should have pretended. But I really, really hated Ethan right then. So I took one swing at him, a wide one that missed his chin by an inch and hit Boone instead. Good God it rang, like a book dropped on a marble floor. Boone went down hard, and after that it was mayhem.

I slipped Oh the diamond, afraid she might catch a wayward punch or dive into the mess to try and break things up, then I curled up into a defensive ball on the ground.

I was kicked twice before the teacher yelled loud enough that everything stopped. As far as the teacher was concerned, we were troublemakers from a different school tangling with a group of over-aggressive football players. The five of us—Milo, me, Oh, Ethan, and Boone—were marched to the office.

I'd taken a kick in the back and a punch to the ear, both of which hurt. Milo had fared better, or so it seemed by the grin he couldn't seem to wipe off his face.

"You think this is funny, son? Well, it's NOT funny," yelled the teacher. Milo stared at the floor.

Oh held an expression of glowing rage, nostrils flared, eyes alive with the desire to slug Ethan in the side of the head with her pink cast. A good look, a sexy one, but also scary, like she could tear your head off if you got in her way.

We were sent to the outer office under the watchful eye of the secretary, where each side glared at the other.

"Enchanted Forest?" whispered Oh. I could barely hear her.

"What?" I whispered back.

"It will make me feel better."

I knew the place. Anyone who'd been in Salem for more than fifteen minutes knew about the Enchanted Forest.

About ten minutes later, we were sent packing with a stern warning not to return. Ethan and Boone were suspended for the day, but only after they met with their coach and told him what had happened. I knew this meant two things: We had a head start, and Ethan and Boone were going to be doing a lot of extra push-ups because of us.

I turned back and saw Ethan being escorted to the gym. The red mark on his head had turned purple and bloomed like an egg right below his hairline. He mouthed the words: *You're dead.* I shook my head. *Actually, I'm about as far from dead as you can imagine.*

"See," said Milo, turning to Oh. "You didn't really want to go to school at South Ridge. We just saved you a lot of time mulling your options."

I pulled Milo aside and left Oh standing near the car.

"Any chance I could borrow your car?" I asked. Every bit of fear I'd had during the past weeks about driving to the coast had vanished. I was ready, right now, to get in a car and drive. Especially if it meant getting time alone with Oh.

"Very funny," said Milo.

"Look, Milo, I *need* your car," I said. "Please."

"You don't even have a license yet. It seems to me we're in enough trouble already."

"I can drive. You know that. I've had a permit for months. I used to drive with Mr. Fielding all the time. I can handle it."

"Is this like some sort of hypnotism trick, 'cause I gotta tell you, it's not working."

Milo tried to walk to his car, but I stopped him with my hand on his shoulder.

"Milo, come on. I really need this right now. Please."

Milo looked at me, then at Oh, then back at me.

"I get it," said Milo, laughing under his breath. "You're trading up. No problem."

"Milo—" I protested.

"No seriously, I'm all good." Milo said. "You want to go for a drive with your girlfriend. Fine by me."

"Milo, come on—" said Oh. "You don't always have to be such a punk about everything."

"No, you come on!" he yelled back at her. "Everything was fine before you showed up."

"She's got nothing to do with it. Maybe you're right; maybe it's this thing—the power, the indestructibility—whatever it is! It's screwing everything up."

"No, that's not true," said Oh. "What we have is a gift."

"Some gift. Ever killed anyone, Oh? I have. It's not as fun as it sounds."

"Now you're just angry—"

"Yeah! I'm angry!"

"Guys..." said Milo, glancing back at the school. The teacher who'd busted us had come outside and was standing with his arms folded across his chest, looking at us like we were three angry dogs that needed to be forcibly removed or shot.

"I'll give you the car," Milo said, his voice calm again, if a little hurt. "Let me drive to the store and park around the block. Then you can have it. Just be careful. You can't protect Oh and yourself at the same time."

"He knows what he's doing," said Oh, sounding more unfriendly with Milo than I was comfortable with.

I hadn't taken the power back from Oh yet, and the strangest thing occurred to me. It didn't hurt. For once, letting her keep it didn't hurt. I looked at her, awestruck by what I was feeling.

We drove to the store and dropped off Milo at the corner. As we passed each other at the busted-up grill of his car, he stopped me and made me catch his eye, then he said something that struck me as very odd.

"We got Kryptonite. It's prowling all around us. You realize that, don't you?"

"Huh?"

Milo shook his head in frustration.

"She's trouble. I know you don't want to hear it, but she is."

"You don't know what you're talking about."

"Don't I?"

I looked through the windshield and saw that Oh was staring at us, looking less tired than she had in days.

"Leave her out of this," I said, crossing back to the driver's side of the car.

"Don't let her control you," Milo said. He'd been quiet before, practically whispering, but this part he said loudly enough for Oh to hear him just fine. Oh turned toward him as I sat down. I couldn't see her expression, but I could imagine it. I was leaving with her, not Milo.

She'd won.

◆　◆　◆

I sat behind the wheel of the parked car thinking about driving. Milo's car was easy: no stick shift and it was gutless. The gas gauge read an eighth of a tank, enough to get us out to the park and back.

"You turn the key," said Oh. "That's how it starts."

I didn't say anything, just sat there breathing heavy, fogging up the cold, wet windshield.

"Have *you* ever driven a car?"

"Yeah, a few times with my dad," Oh said casually. "Easy."

I'd lost my nerve and couldn't do it. I couldn't so much as turn the stupid key with my stupid, clammy fingers.

"Let's do that, then. Let's have you drive us out there."

"You okay?"

I got out of the car without answering, and by the time I opened the passenger door, Oh had lifted herself over the cup holders into the driver's seat.

We drove the back roads, avoiding the freeway, Oh totally focused on the task at hand and me sucking in a breath around every corner. I kept looking at her, trying to remember who she was when I'd met her. Vibrant, that was the best word I could think of to describe Ophelia James the first time I'd seen her pink cast. Even in a good mood, she was so different now. Paler skin, deeper eyes, a short fuse.

I sat there thinking how strange it was that she was still the most beautiful girl I'd ever seen.

"Slow down. It's wet out here."

"What are you, my mom?"

We were on a curvy, out-of-the-way road with wet trees and moss and slick boulders in every direction. Oh stopped the car on the shoulder and rolled down her window. The smell of wet earth, thick and healthy, flooded my lungs.

206

"It's okay you're afraid to drive," she said, looking at me. "If I'd gone through what you did with Mr. Fielding on the way to the coast, I'd be afraid to get into a car at all." She touched my cheek with the warm palm of her good hand. "It's okay. *We're* okay. You don't have to carry the weight of the world by yourself. The power makes you… I don't know, do crazy things sometimes. I can help you carry this burden around. I like helping you. It makes me happy."

She leaned in and we kissed. I don't know how many minutes passed, one or ten or somewhere in between. It was timeless and perfect.

That is, until I rested my hand on her knee.

"I have to pee," Oh informed me, pulling back. It made me feel like I'd moved too fast.

"Can you get your pants down with that cast or do you need some help out there?"

"I think I can manage it."

She disappeared into the woods, and I drank in the cool air, listening to the sound of tires on wet pavement as a car drove by. Then I finally got up the courage and slid over into the driver's seat. We were on a country road, about as back-road as it gets, and it was time to get this over with. She'd left the keys in the ignition, and I had Milo's old beater running again before she returned.

The door opened on the passenger side and Oh peeked in hesitantly, looking more energetic than before.

"You sure you're ready for this, Mario?"

"Yeah, I got it."

"Next stop, the Crooked House," said Oh.

The Enchanted Forest is what Disneyland might very well have become if it had been opened in Salem, Oregon. But Mr. Tofte, the visionary who created the Enchanted Forest, didn't have Southern California weather and millions of people on his side. Turns out those things make a lot of difference when you're starting a theme park.

"Did you just grab my butt?" I asked. Oh was behind me and we were standing in the claustrophobic interior of a mine where the mechanical puppets of the seven dwarves were busily searching for gold.

"I did. A little flabby," she answered.

I tensed my butt cheeks as hard as I could.

"Try it again. I've been working out."

She walked ahead of me and leaned over the rail, where neon-colored water poured into pools of light and little men whistled while they worked. When we came out the other side, the world was a forgotten forest, filled with giant trees and a rolling path.

"God I love this place," said Oh, twirling around and breathing in the moist air. It was nice seeing her so happy and carefree. I promised myself I'd bring her back every week.

Misty rain caught in the trees overhead and pooled until the trees couldn't hold it anymore. Great blobs of water plopped to the forest floor and we walked, hoodies pulled over our heads, soaked and leaning into each other.

We'd gone through the Storybook Lane portion of the

park, where fairy tales came to life with slides and crawl-spaces and crooked walkways. Humpty Dumpty, Little Miss Muffet, the Three Little Bears—it was surprisingly fun and a perfect date. Lots of places to grab a rock-hard butt cheek.

We held hands all the way through the English Village and bought cinnamon churros from a vendor on the wood-slat streets of Western Town. The Enchanted Forest gets better as you go, which, I suppose, is part of its charm.

There are not a lot of lines at noon on a Friday in October, and an hour later we'd ridden the bobsled four times, gotten soaked on the log ride, and endured the Challenge of Mondor (don't ask). There was only one attraction left, and it was by different accounts either the best or stupidest one in the whole park.

"Are you ready?" Oh asked nervously.

"You do realize people go in there all the time and never come out."

"You'll protect me," she said, pulling me up the hill toward a huge run-down psycho house sitting dismally under the sinking sky.

The Haunted House wasn't so much scary as it was dis-orienting. It was big, with lots of puppets that moved and staircases to go up and down. There was just a skeleton crew running the winter season, and the guy taking the tickets out front was, I'm quite sure, the only employee within a hundred yards of the front door. Once you went in, getting out was not his problem.

"Don't screw around in there," he said, obviously bored.

"I'll do my best," I offered, and then Oh pulled hard on my arm and we were inside.

She held my hand tightly in the gathering gloom of the entrance as the door shut behind us and everything went dark. I expected her to giggle or try to scare me, but all I heard was her breathing heavier than she had been, like she'd run up a flight of stairs and was trying to catch her breath.

"Everything okay?" I asked, but she didn't answer. She kept pulling me deeper into the darkness, past walls of skulls and floating plastic bats. We were in the darkest part of the Haunted House, truly pitch-black with tiny lights down long hallways, when Oh let go of my hand.

"Jacob Fielding?" I heard her half whisper in the dark.

"Yes?" I answered, trying to figure out which direction her voice was coming from.

"I love you."

I heard her steps running away. I just stood there, wobbly legged in the dark. I should have answered her. I should have said I loved her back, but my head was spinning. Something wasn't right. Why was she running away from me?

I felt my chest and realized, in a flash, that I didn't have the power. *She* had the power. She'd had it all morning, and it hadn't tried to make its way back to me.

That could only mean one thing: Something about the power had changed. But what? Had it chosen a new home? And why was she running from me? I began to feel a creeping sense of doubt as Milo's warning repeated in my head.

We got Kryptonite. It's prowling all around us. You real-ize that, don't you?

A hand grabbed my arm and I turned, expecting to see Oh and to laugh off my paranoid train of thought. But the hand was far too big to be Oh's.

It spun me around, fast and hard, and there in the blue shadow of a plastic bat floating overhead was Reginald Boone.

"Hey, Boone," I said numbly. The fear of being man-handled by a linebacker gripped me like an iron vise.

"You and your friends should have stayed where you belonged," said Boone, anger rising in his voice.

The fact that I'd never taken the power back from Oh in the South Ridge parking lot filled my mind as his knuckles hit my eye. Taking the power back from Oh never occurred to me. I loved her, everything was going haywire, she might be in trouble, and I didn't trust what she might do.

Boone's fist turned the darkness of the Haunted House into sparks of color as it hit my face and my head exploded in pain.

"Ethan!" yelled Boone. "I'm done here, man."

The world was spinning. The only thing I could focus on was that name. *Ethan.* He was somewhere in the dark, and so was Oh.

"Stay put, loser," Boone said, pushing me down on the floor with the heel of his shoe as he took off.

"Oh," I said, but it came out quiet, a crackling whis-per. I shook my head, and my brain sloshed back and forth miserably. Clawing at the wall, I managed to find my way back onto my feet.

I couldn't take it back. What good would it do anyway? I was like the heart attack victim, already hit with the punch. The damage was done.

"Oh," I yelled, my voice returning, but still there was no answer. Stumbling around a haunted house is incredibly frustrating when you're buckled over in pain. I kept hitting my shoulders against corners and bumping my head on things I couldn't see.

Then I heard Ethan laughing. God, I hated the sound of Ethan's howler. It echoed off the walls, filling the entire house as if it had been recorded and piped in on speakers.

I covered the eye that had been hit, and it made it easier to see. The sting remained but the blurriness was gone as I swung narrowly around a corner and started up a set of creaking stairs.

Ethan's laugh hit a high point and abruptly ended as I reached the top of a stairway and turned down a dark corridor. There was a choking sound, awful and wet, and I screamed Oh's name as she came into view.

The end of the hall was lit with an orange bulb that made the corner look soaked in blood. But Oh wasn't being choked by Ethan or pinned down with her face on the floor. No.

She was hovering over *him*, her hands wrapped around *his* neck.

Ethan couldn't stop her. He punched her in the head over

and over again, but Oh wouldn't let go. She was a Dober-
man, lock-jawed and furious, and it didn't look to me like
she had it within herself to let him live.

She was killing him.

I screamed at her again to let go, approaching her from
the side, but I might as well have been a ghost for all she
noticed. Oh was utterly possessed by bloodlust.

Ethan's swings went rubbery and soft, the oxygen running out as his arms moved like fins on a half-dead fish.

I closed my eyes and wearily said the only words that
could save Ethan's life.

You are indestructible.

Oh's breath caught in her throat, and it reminded me
of when someone is stabbed in the back in the movies and
they react with this sort of *Oh my God that hurt and I'm
totally dead.*

"Let him go," I whispered. "You're going to kill him."

Oh still had a hold of Ethan's neck, staring blank-eyed
down into his fluttering eyes.

"Oh," I repeated. "You have to stop. You're going to
kill Ethan."

Oh's breathing returned, choppy and hysterical. She
started to cry, glancing back and forth between me and
the life she was about to end. Ethan had gone limp on the
floor, but I could *feel* his breathing beginning to return to
normal.

Oh let go and stood against the wall wiping her hands
on her jeans as if they were covered in blood. I leaned down

and slapped Ethan across the face, thinking it might revive him. But it didn't. He just lay there in the dark, the purple bump on his forehead staring up at me like a third eye.

"Ethan!" I yelled. "Get your sorry ass up right now!"

I pumped his chest with my fist twice and shook him back and forth. Yeah, I'm not exactly a doctor. Finally, mercifully, he stirred. Like a boxer knocked out in the tenth round, battered and bruised, he slowly opened his eyes.

"Fielding? What the hell?"

"For once I'm really glad to see you," I said, standing back up and putting out a hand to help him off the floor. Ethan slapped my hand away, kicking at my legs as he crawled closer to the corner. He looked like he was in shock and maybe couldn't remember exactly what had happened.

I took the power back before he could use any of the energy he had left to kick my ass, and this time I was surer than ever it was a living thing passing back and forth between us. The lion had emotions, or something like them, because this time it wasn't afraid or angry or clawing to get back in. I felt heavier at my center, stronger, like I was an iron shell holding a contented little beast in my chest.

"Ethan, dude, just calm down. It's over. You're fine."

There was recognition in his eyes as he remembered what had gone down. He stared at me, bewildered.

"Listen to me, okay?" I said in my calmest voice. "She's a hell of a lot tougher than she looks. You just tangled with the wrong girl, that's all."

"What happened to your eye?" he asked, touching his neck and feeling the bruises starting to form.

"Boone," I said. "My face beat the crap out of his hand."

Ethan laughed very softly. I could tell he was starting to calm down.

"Damn, that girl is strong. All you guys are. It's freakin' crazy. Where'd she go?"

I looked up over my shoulder where Oh should have been, but she wasn't there. I yelled for her but got no answer.

"This is it, Ethan," I said, turning my eye on him. I had to end this right now, before I went searching for Oh. "This is over. I'll keep Oh and Milo away, but you gotta stop this."

"Deal," said Ethan. He stood up with a painful sigh and looked in every direction.

"You know the way out?"

"Follow me." I had no idea how to get out, but there was no way I was leaving Ethan alone with Oh still missing. The last thing I wanted was the two of them bumping into each other in the dark. I put my head down, felt the blood pushing against my swollen eye.

You are indestructible.

It hurt more than ever. It wasn't like letting the power out anymore, it was like reaching in and tearing it out of my chest while it dug in with its claws and tried to hold on. It hurt so bad I stumbled in the dark and groaned like someone had kicked me in the groin.

"You okay, man?" asked Ethan.

I kept walking, half buckled over but feeling better by the second, nodding that I was fine.

I probably shouldn't have given it back to her, but I couldn't help myself. She could be anywhere, doing anything. I had to protect her.

♦ ♦ ♦

I never did find Oh. I searched everywhere in the Haunted House until the manager came in and turned up the lights. Oh wasn't there, but the attendant was sure ready to get rid of me. The swollen eye gave away the fight, and I was not so much asked to leave as escorted off the premises.

When I got back to the car, Oh's longboard was gone. She'd brought it along, but they didn't allow skating on the grounds. I yelled Oh's name out the window of Milo's car all the way home. It was freezing with the windows down, but I didn't care. Around every corner I hoped I'd see her hitchhiking or riding her longboard down a slick, curvy road, but she was nowhere.

When I got inside Coffin Books, Milo's mom was sitting behind the counter in her La-Z-Boy, chatting up a customer. She only ever worked days until four, so I didn't know her all that well.

"I haven't seen you for a couple weeks," she said. "Avoiding me on purpose?"

"Is Milo here?" I asked, wholly unable to start a

conversation with an adult in the wake of what had happened. My swelled eye was hidden behind a pair of barely operational sunglasses I'd found in Milo's glove box.

"Up there," she said, pointing to the loft with a stabbing finger. She went back to her conversation, but I could feel her narrow eyes on my back as I passed the rows of books.

"He's in a bad mood."

The voice came from down the long, thin row of horror novels to my left. It was the biggest section in the store, and the weirdest. Unlike the other straight aisles of books teetering at the top with overstock paperbacks, the horror section was a zigzagging mess, gobbling up space wherever it could be found.

"That you, Mr. Coffin?" I asked, though I knew the answer.

I crept back along the narrow shelves. Mr. Coffin appeared from around one of the sharp corners, scaring me half to death.

"He's in a bad mood," he repeated. "Go easy on him."

"This place is scary enough without you appearing out of nowhere."

"You look terrible," he said, trying to see past the sunglasses. "Everything okay?"

"Yeah, yeah, fine. Everything's fine."

I started to leave, but turned back to Mr. C, remembering something.

"Did I see you at the church the other day?"

He began pulling and pushing books on the nearest shelf, averting his eyes.

"I go over there once in a while, talk to the old guys."

All I could think was yeah, right, like anyone wants to sit in the church house kitchen drinking bad coffee talking to a bunch of old priests.

"Whatever you say," I said, shrugging my shoulders.

Mr. Coffin looked at me, then the floor. He wasn't great at confrontations.

"I don't know, Jacob, watching you three has been a little unnerving."

"What do you mean?"

Oh crap, another adult on to us.

"Milo's moody, you're moody, and that girl—what's her name, Ophelia?—she comes around without you two lately, picks some pretty dark material. She hovers around too, longer than most. And she doesn't look...well."

I was surprised to hear about Oh visiting Coffin Books by herself. She hadn't told me or Milo.

"We're fine, Mr. Coffin, really. Everyone's just tired of the rain and the schoolwork is all. You know how it is."

Mr. Coffin nodded, but he wasn't buying it, I could tell.

"If you say so."

I was about to go when he looked at me sideways, like Miss Pines liked to do, and asked about Mr. Fielding's box.

"What's that got to do with anything?" I snapped.

"Maybe a lot more than you'd think," Mr. Coffin

answered, giving me a penetrating look. "Nothing, that's— look, forget I mentioned it. We're worried about you and for my son, that's it. That's all there is."

He turned and disappeared around a shelf before I could respond.

I climbed the ladder and found Milo staring into a paperback copy of *The Castle of Otranto*. The book was a sort of safety blanket for him. I'd seen it in his back pocket, on the floor in the backseat of his car, and floating around in his backpack.

"What's new at the castle?" I asked, flopping down in a chair beside him and hoping he'd pull his nose out of the book and talk to me.

"Same old thing," he said. "I like it that way. Predictable."

"Milo." I stopped short, not sure what to say as I took his crappy sunglasses off. Then I just blurted it out. "I'm in some trouble. I need your help."

Milo set the book on the table and leaned forward, eyebrows raised at the sight of my bulging black eye.

"Whoa. How'd that happen?"

"I'm fine—it's no big deal—just tell me—"

"She's fine. That's what you came here for, right?"

"How do you know? Did she call you?"

Milo shook his head.

"Where is she?"

Milo sighed and turned back to the book. I didn't begrudge him for it. Sometimes I wished I didn't have to deal with the real world either. I'd chosen a girl over my best friend, that was obvious, and now I was coming to him for help. He was under no obligation.

"She texted me," he began. "Said she'd really rather not be bothered for a while. You must have really impressed her."

He looked me in the face again.

"She do that to you?"

"No, it was Boone."

I recounted the scene in the Haunted House, right down to the part where Oh just about killed Ethan.

"Jesus," he said. "She's even farther out there than I thought."

"Ethan's fine," I said, wincing at the memory of Oh's crazed face. "But you're right. I think she's in real trouble. We have to find her."

"Nope, *you* have to find her. Good luck with that."

"Are you hearing me?" I raised my voice, then imagined Mr. Coffin standing under the loft and went back to a near whisper.

"She needs us to help her. We got into this mess together, right? We all participated and now something's gone wrong. I know you're pissed about me and Oh. It just happened. It wasn't anyone's fault."

He shook his head and fanned the pages in his book.

"She said to tell you she was fine," he offered half-heartedly. "She's at home with her mom, said she needed a couple of days to figure some things out."

Are those things about me? Damn. The concern I'd had for Ethan—and what I'd glimpsed in Oh—seemed to vanish, and for some sick reason, all I could think about was how bummed I was that my trip to the coast with Oh was off.

My true character was coming out, and it wasn't super amazing, awesome, and great. It sucked.

"You think she was telling the truth?" I asked.

"How the hell should I know? And stop putting me between you two."

"Okay, okay—sorry."

"Look, man, if you're here for a steak to put on that eye, I can't help you," Milo said, digging in his heels and flopping back in his chair. "You got what you came for."

I debated with myself, thinking about Oh, Milo, and everything that had happened.

"There are some things I need to tell you, Milo. Not Oh or Father Tim or anyone else, just you."

Milo's knees swung in and out as he pretended to read something I was sure he'd read ten times before.

"I'm sorry, okay?" I said. "This whole thing has been insane. I made some mistakes. We all did."

Still nothing but the back cover of an old book.

"Come on, man, cut me some slack here. I'm trying. I screwed up with Oh, but she's important to me. And I think she's experiencing something totally different than we are. I think the power is doing something to her."

"Like what?"

I didn't answer, because I truly had no idea.

"What are these things you need to tell me?" asked Milo from behind the book.

"It's complicated," I offered, trying to buy some time.

"It always is."

I decided to try some humor and see if it would help. "Will you go on a date with me?"

I couldn't see his face, but I was pretty sure he was starting to crack.

"I promise you won't be sorry. I'll be gentle."

He put the book down and shook his head at me. Not the smile I'd hoped for.

"She's dangerous. You know that, right?"

We sat in silence and I thought about Oh finding Ethan or Boone and what might happen, but I was even more worried about something that felt far worse.

"What if she tries to hurt herself?" I asked, staring at the table.

"I've been thinking the same thing. She's kind of got that look."

Milo glanced out over the store, leaned in closer to the table. "She got the power?"

I nodded.

"Well, at least we know she can't get hurt. Kind of risky though, know what I mean?"

I nodded, then sat there for a minute, thinking the worst, hoping she was home sleeping and dreaming.

"Did I mention you're going to have to drive on our date?" I asked.

"Cheap bastard."

◆ ◆ ◆

Milo took me back to the church house, and I lay on my bed and thought about the date I'd planned that wouldn't happen. That, and what it had looked like to see her getting her head bashed in while she choked Ethan.

I finally got up the nerve to text her.

Talked to M. are you sure you're OK?

A few minutes later, I got a response.

I'm good. tired. need to think about some things.

Like why you tried to kill Ethan?

Me: *You're scaring me a little bit.*

A three-minute pause, which made me *insane*. I picked up Mr. Fielding's Zippo and flicked it alive, letting the flame dance in front of my eyes.

Oh: *No need to be. I'm not coming after you.*

That was some seriously black humor, plus avoiding the point.

Me: *Just saying, you might've really hurt the guy.*

Oh: *Wouldn't have gone that far.*

Me: *You sure?*

Pushing it, but as long as she was talking...

Oh: *I think you should leave me alone now.*

The flame from Mr. Fielding's Zippo had gone out, and I flicked it four or five times but it wouldn't come back to life.

Me: *I want to see you.*

Oh: *Take it back.*

Me: *Huh?*

Oh: *You know what I mean.*

Me: *I can't.*

Two minutes later.

Me: *Oh?*

Five minutes later.

Me: *Oh?*

She was gone.

I set my phone down and went to my desk for the lighter fluid so I could reload Mr. Fielding's Zippo and get it working again. The metal casing was really stuck on there tightly, like it hadn't been taken off in a long while. It made a thick scratching sound when it finally slid free. I turned over the inside of the lighter so I could pour fluid into the felt.

The part I held in my hand had this thin sheath of metal and a thick, smoke-stained center that looked like burnt marshmallows. I touched the inside, the felt that was dry and soft. Except it wasn't all soft. There was a rigid center, hard and firm, and when I pushed the felt off to the sides, the rounded top of a small piece of metal appeared. When I touched it the metal moved, and I was worried I might have jogged something loose and the old lighter wouldn't work right anymore. I got the piece of metal between my fingernails and drew it out, small and silver.

It was not the kind of thing you'd expect to find inside a Zippo lighter.

If I'd never met Mr. Coffin I might have thought, *What's a key doing in a place like this?* If I'd never seen Mr. Fielding glance in that certain place at the coast, like he'd hidden something there, I might have thought, *A key? What the hell's it for?*

But I knew what the key was for just as sure as Father Frank would make terrible coffee in the morning. The key was for the box.

Best I could figure, Mr. Fielding had probably always owned the key, but maybe the box was stolen or lost. He'd hired Mr. Coffin to find the box, the Isengrim, letters, manuscripts, a lot of things.

My phone vibrated three times where it lay on my bed.

Her: *Take it back.*

It was the last I heard from Oh all night.

FOURTEEN HOURS TO MIDNIGHT

SATURDAY, OCTOBER 20TH

The next morning Milo picked me up and we drove to the Oregon coast. Along the winding road, lined with forests in every shade of green, we started piecing some things together.

"Think about it this way," Milo said, touching the buttons on his iPod. He'd drifted into a Led Zeppelin phase, and we were deep into "Houses of the Holy." Road trip music, he'd called it. "Something's happening to Oh that's not happening to either of us."

"I get that part, believe me. But why?"

"Well, what are the obvious things? She's a girl, we're guys. She's been more affected by the stress of it than either of us, losing sleep and stuff. Maybe that's something. And she's had the power more than me by a long shot. Maybe it's like poison."

"If it were poison, I'd be dead."

"Not necessarily. I mean think about it, this thing started out inside *you*, not her. Maybe you're, I don't know, immune somehow, and she's not."

It was a curious idea that might have a little merit.

"I don't think it matters that she's a girl," I went on. "But I see what you're saying about how much more into it she is and how she's always angling to get it."

"Who was first?" asked Milo.

"What do you mean, first?"

"I mean, who'd you give it to first? Her, right? You wrote it on her cast, remember?"

I nodded, sipping from a cup of Starbucks I'd brought along.

"Could be she was first and now...dang, I don't know."

I picked up where Milo left off.

"No, wait, I think that could be something. What are we really doing, when you get right down to it?"

Milo didn't answer, so I went on.

"If we've saved a life, we've prevented a death. But in the grand scheme of things, you can't keep preventing death, for like, ever, right? It's like throwing off the natural order of things. Death still has to have its moment. I tried to get into this with Father Tim, but he wasn't much help."

Milo jumped on my train of thought. "So...are you asking yourself something like, if death was gonna come to town but didn't, where the hell did it go instead?"

"Yeah, I guess I am. And there's something else. When I have the power, it feels darker and deadlier all the time, and when I give it to someone else, say the guy at the bank, it tries to claw its way back in. But—"

"Wait a minute. Back up. Say that again? The diamond feels dark? *Deadly?*"

"Yeah…I never mentioned it before, but I think I know why. It's been small shifts toward a deadlier feeling over time, adding up. It's like I've been lulled into it, I guess."

"So you never talked about that. The power of indestructibility feels deadly. Pretty ironic."

"Except now, when I give it to Oh. Then it doesn't want to come back."

Milo stared out the rain-streaked windshield, moving his chin to the beat of "Over the Hills and Far Away."

"So…it likes being there, I guess. Maybe because you gave it to her first, and this power, whatever it is, just keeps going back. Every time Death doesn't find its eternal resting place, it's going to go somewhere else. What if Oh is that place?"

"Dude, that's sick. I don't get it. She's not dead."

"Maybe she wants to be."

I was stunned to silence.

"No, seriously. Maybe Mr. Fielding never gave it to anyone until he gave it to you. Think about it. He passes the power to you, then he dies. He's gone and you have it. One life ends, another continues on. But what we're doing isn't like that. You've passed that thing all over the place like a flu bug. Who knows what kind of rift in the death-life continuum you've created?"

Milo was going all comic book on me, but he might have been onto something.

"And so the question would be what? How much death can Oh carry around before it drives her insane? Very nice."

Milo shrugged and stared out the window.

"Hear me out. Think of it as an animal, like this black lion you keep imagining. It lives in you, you're like its cave, right? And you send it out to protect someone. The death comes calling and the black lion picks it up and carries it back to you, but now he's home. He doesn't want a rotting ugly death hanging around his cave stinking up the place— he wants to get rid of it. So where does he put it? The same place he always puts it."

"Inside Oh?" I whispered. "Man, that is so crazy, Milo. It makes sense for, like, half a second, and then I totally lose it again."

"Could be the black lion is as confused as we are. You send him over to Oh, and he expects you to be gone when he turns back, like Mr. Fielding was gone. But no, you're still standing there! Now he's like—which one is home?— it's you, man, you're his home. And Oh? That's important to him, too. That's where he goes to unload his burdens."

"Dude, that was heavy, but pretty cool."

"I know. It's also probably a load of horseshit."

"True."

Milo switched off the iPod with a flick of his thumb and stared at me despite the fact that we were doing fifty around a wide two-lane turn. Time to unload a secret.

"Eighteen is a magic number," I said. "It's when you get to vote or join the army. Or get an inheritance."

"Tell me more," said Milo, eyes back on the road as a semitruck blasted by and sprayed his windshield with standing road water. Everything outside turned murky as the wipers tried to catch up.

"Father Tim hasn't been going to Seattle to beg for money. He's been working out a plan for what the school is going to do when I graduate."

"What happens when you graduate?"

"They have to take care of me until then. No more foster homes, that was part of the deal. Once I'm gone though, they get ten."

"Ten—ten—ten...you mean *ten?*"

"Yeah, I mean ten million."

"Holy freakin' Schlotzsky, Jacob! Why didn't you tell me? Ten *million?* The whole place isn't worth a fraction of that."

"Thank you for not swearing. It means a lot. You want some of my money, don't you?"

"Sounds to me like it's the school's money, Richie Rich."

I laughed for the first time on our trip and sipped my coffee. "First off, the will actually said I couldn't tell anyone about *any* of the money. Not the part for the school or what was left for me, so I'm taking a huge risk telling you. That's the rule I was referring to. Who knows, maybe Mr. Fielding left people behind who could screw this up, I don't know. But you have to keep a lid on it. No one can know about it."

"How much do you get?" asked Milo.

"Enough," I said.

"Come on! Don't hold out on me, man! How much?"

"There are a lot of zeros, that's all I'm saying. He left me everything else. There was no one, not even a distant relative or a friend. Just me and the school."

"I can't believe my best friend is super rich. Incredible."

"When I turn eighteen, we'll throw a party and I'll buy you a new front bumper. For now just forget I ever told you, because nothing's going to change for a while."

We were coming to a place on the trip where I was going to ask Milo to pull over, but now that the time had come, I wasn't sure if I could do it. I sipped my coffee and Milo tried to get the inheritance amount out of me. I wasn't going to tell him, maybe not ever, but it was an insane number. Lately I'd actually had some thoughts about what I could use the money for, at least some of it, but we were coming to the spot where I needed to have Milo stop.

"Pull over," I said.

"Gotta pee?" he said, looking at my empty Starbucks cup. "That's why I don't drink those things on a road trip."

I didn't answer as the car swung around another wide, soft turn through an old-growth forest. He pulled to the shoulder and started messing with his iPod again.

"Come on," I said, opening my door.

"I think you're taking this whole date thing a little far. I'm not that interested in helping you take a leak."

I leaned back into the car, felt the rain on my neck.

"I don't have to pee, Milo. Just come with me."

Milo shrugged and turned off the car, then we walked together in the rain. We'd come up short by about thirty yards.

"This is where it happened," I said, pointing to a stand of trees up in the distance.

Milo didn't say anything but I knew he got it. He understood we'd arrived at the place where Mr. Fielding was killed. We reached the group of trees, both of us dripping wet and shivering. They were something else. The trunks were spotted green with moss, shooting overhead into canopies of branches against an iron gray sky.

"We used to drive around a lot. It was just this thing we did. Long drives that always ended with a big breakfast. Sometimes it was an all-day thing on a Saturday because we kept picking places that were far away."

"I know. You've told me like a thousand times," said Milo, but he knew it meant a lot to me. "It sounds cool."

"If we were on a back road somewhere or he was feeling especially tired because it was a long way to where we were going he would...well, you know..."

Now that I'd come to a secret truth, I couldn't bring myself to say it.

"What? Pull off the road and take a nap?" asked Milo. "What did he do?"

I took a long breath of fresh air so full of life it made me light-headed. I thought seriously about running all the way home. Could I make it? If I ran all day, could I outrun the pain like I'd always done? I'd done a lot of running in my day. Sometimes it had been the right thing to do, like when I saw a gun or a needle, but this time was different. The pain had caught me on the side of the road, and I couldn't get away.

"Once in a while he let me drive the car," I said quietly.

"Dude, this is old news. You've told me all this stuff before."

My best friend looked at me then, and I could tell he'd finally figured it out. I was sure he'd hate me.

"Don't say what I think you're going to say," said Milo.

I wasn't thinking anymore, I was just talking.

"We were going to the Oregon coast for breakfast at this place called the Pig 'N Pancake," I said. "It's a long drive."

I saw the flash of understanding pass over Milo's face. His mouth hung open, and all the muscles around his eyes went slack under wet skin. Everyone at Holy Cross knew the story. We'd been driving to the coast on a rainy day, swerved off the road, slammed into a giant old-growth tree. But that hadn't been the whole truth.

I'd been thinking a lot about Father Tim's words earlier in the week, when we were in his office and I almost choked on my toast.

Sometimes a person will share mistakes more openly with a friend than with a priest. You understand what I mean?

But I couldn't do it. I couldn't get myself to say the words. I'd held them in too long and turned mute on the subject. It was Milo, pal that he was, who said what I couldn't say, the thing I'd expected to keep secret forever.

"You were driving when the accident happened, weren't you?"

I didn't answer him, didn't have to. That's what made it cool, and maybe what Father Tim had meant. Milo was the friend who said things I couldn't say for myself.

I stood in silence, gazing out at the trees, and felt an awful tightening in my lungs, remembering the sound of approaching police cars as I stumbled around in a daze after the accident. Mr. Fielding and I were both blown through the windshield and thrown at least twenty feet from the car. At that point, it was impossible to say who was driving, so I lied. When they asked, I said it was him, not me, behind the wheel; I couldn't quite believe that it *had* been me. Until this very moment, I hadn't been able to truly even accept it.

My chest started heaving, but I couldn't cry. No way I was doing that. I never cried in front of anyone. But the rain was falling and my face was already wet. I stared up into a thundering sky and my throat narrowed.

So, Milo knew that I'd killed Mr. Fielding. It was an accident, sure, but it didn't matter to me. It would never matter. I was a killer, always would be. That's how I felt about it.

Milo put an arm around me. He didn't say a word, and I couldn't be totally sure if tears were sliding down my cheeks or not. All I knew was that I hurt like I hadn't hurt before, and I was glad my best friend was with me.

♦ ♦ ♦

An hour later we arrived in Lincoln City, a tourist town on the Pacific with a ceaseless wind and car-sized black rocks scattered on the beaches. Everything felt old and seaworthy: chipped paint storefronts, monstrous docks with timber pylons, countless fishing boats, and gray-bearded sailors in search of chowder and a beer. Southern Cal it was not.

"So this is the hangout? The pipe place you've been telling me about since day one?" Milo asked, staring at the sign over the door. *Sir Walter Raleigh's.*

"That it is," I answered, sliding a key from my hip pocket. I thought of all the things I'd planned to do with Oh but didn't get to do as the door opened and an old, familiar smell floated out of the pipe shop. Milo hadn't been inside Sir Walter Raleigh's, but I'd told him about it a few times, how me and Mr. Fielding would come here together.

"Let me guess," said Milo, blasting past me into the small space. "He gave you this place, too."

"Technically, it belongs to Father Tim until I'm of age, but yeah, it's pretty much mine."

"Who pays the rent?"

"Nobody. The whole building is mine."

"Good God, man, you're a tycoon."

I slid in behind one of the two counters, not ready to get what I'd come for just yet. The counters ran waist-high along both sides of the store, glass tops covering rows of pipes and lighters. At the far end sat a bar made from a boat rail. There were three stools and Milo sat on one of them.

"I do love that smell," said Milo, breathing in a giant whiff of pipe tobacco.

"You know, this place was only open on Saturdays," I said, setting my cell phone on the bar and fishing two pipes and a lighter out from under the counter. "Eleven Saturdays, that's how many I spent here. He'd open the shop, then give me a twenty and send me down to the beach for crab rings. By the time I got back to Sir Walter's, there were always two or three old men sitting on the stools, smoking their pipes and talking about how developers were ruining Lincoln City."

I leaned back and opened a sliding glass door where the cookie jars of tobacco were kept. Each glass container had a label, and I chose the smoothest blend Mr. Fielding carried. A rookie blend, as he liked to call it. I filled the pipes, handed one to Milo, and we lit them. Gray smoke filled the room, and a fan whirled to life over our heads, sucking the smoke into the chilled air outside.

"Fancy," said Milo.

"The smoke sets it off, keeps things from getting too stuffy in here. It's like when you go by a Burger King and they're pumping the smell of French fries into the air. Mr. Fielding loved the fact that ten minutes after the fan went on, someone showed up at the front door with a pipe in his hand, looking for a conversation."

"So some old dudes are about to show up, that what you're telling me?"

I hadn't thought of that and leaned over, turning off the fan with the manual switch.

We smoked our pipes, tested some of the spendier Zippos.

"Why are we here?" asked Milo.

"Hopefully for some answers, but I don't know for sure."

I reached back into the cooler and pulled out one of the glass jars. It was marked Captain Black.

"He said something once, I guess it must have been the fifth or sixth time he brought me here. I didn't think much of it at the time."

"And..." said Milo, sucking on his pipe and trying without success to blow a smoke ring.

"If something happens to me and you don't know what to do, come back here, okay?"

"What's that supposed to mean?"

"Mr. Fielding's words, not mine. He was talking about the future, about what might happen if he ever died. And he kept looking at this jar of Captain Black, like he'd put something there for me to find. You know, when you get that feeling someone is hiding something? You're just so sure of it—"

"Yeah, I know what you mean," said Milo, looking at me as if I'd been a good example of exactly what I was talking about.

"It was always in the back of my mind, figured it was money or a parting note about how much he'd enjoyed my company or something."

"But now you're not so sure?"

"Yeah, now I'm not so sure. I think it has something to do with this ability I have. I think it was a secret he didn't want anyone else to know about."

I reached in where the glass jar had been and felt around with my hand. There was a ledge there, at the back, that dropped down a few inches.

"Anything?" asked Milo, sitting up in his chair and leaning over the bar with the pipe between his teeth. He looked a fair amount like Popeye.

I had my fingers around something kind of small, which made me wonder if I'd gotten it right. I'd expected a decent-size box. I don't know why, Mr. Coffin never said, and I didn't ask.

"I've seen that before," said Milo, surprised as I was at the small thing I'd uncovered.

"No way."

"Yeah, huh...my dad had it."

"You know he tracked down a lot of stuff for Mr. Fielding?"

"Course I know. My dad finds stuff for a lot of people, collectors and stuff. I do remember he was into that box though. It didn't have a key."

The box was the size, shape, and weight of a three-hundred-page hardback book, with a keyhole on one of the long edges. The thing was old, had to be a serious antique.

"Should we bust it open?" asked Milo. "Maybe there's a million nickels inside."

I rolled my eyes and dug my hand in my pocket, pulling out the small silver key from the lighter.

"You're kidding me," said Milo. His pipe had gone out and he set it in an ashtray, waving me over the bar. I set the box down carefully, looked at my watch.

"How about if I open it while you drive back toward home," I said, feeling more isolated than I liked on the farthest shore of Oregon. "If we need to see Oh, we're going to want her close by."

If what we were about to see could help me trust Oh again, if it could fix whatever had gone wrong, I wanted to be as close to her as I could.

Milo smirked and set the pipe down in the ashtray. "Let me ask you something."

"What?"

242

"How long have you and I known each other?"

I thought back to our first encounter the summer before at Coffin Books. "I don't know, seven months, eight?"

"Yeah, about that. And how long did you know Mr. Fielding?"

"Like a year. What's your point?"

"Know anyone else that long?"

I thought a second, then another, then really tried to look back. "No, he was the longest. Unless you include my mom when I was really little and a couple foster kids I haven't seen in a while."

"Well, I guess that makes sense, then."

"What makes sense?"

"I'm just thinking to myself, you've known Ophelia James for thirteen days. I counted. Me? You've known me longer than almost anyone, and we're best friends."

"I can't explain it, okay? I think I was in love with that girl the moment I saw her. It doesn't feel like just thirteen days. It feels like there's everything that came before I met Oh and then everything that came after."

Milo nodded thoughtfully, picked up the pipe again.

"I see what you mean, but I don't think she wants to see either one of us right now," said Milo.

"Maybe not. But—"

"Dude, just open it. Driving won't make it any easier." Milo smacked his lips. "Wait, before you do that—this crab shack got any water?"

I knew there were cans of 7UP sitting at the bottom of the cooler and pulled two of them out, snapping the tops and setting them on the counter.

"You're a regular bartender. Don't expect a big tip, Mr. Moneybags."

"Mr. Fielding said 7UP was the ultimate pipe-smoking beverage. The fizz and the sugar soothed his throat and gave his pipe a sweet flavor."

"Bottoms up," said Milo, chugging down half the contents of his can in four giant gulps. It was followed by a wet, smoky burp.

I sat down on my barstool, spinning the key between my fingers. In the moment that I hesitated to open the box, my phone started vibrating on the bar and Milo picked it up. It wasn't a text, because it kept vibrating over and over. Someone was calling.

"It's Oh."

"No way," I said, grabbing my phone from Milo and clicking the call to life. Oh started talking before I could say hello.

"Are you near a computer? You *have* to be."

"Um, hi, Oh, how are you?"

"Tell me you are, Jacob. Someone's in trouble."

I could imagine her hunched over the police scanner, eyes drained of life.

"Look, Oh, I'm not sure—"

"It's a kid, Jacob. A *kid*. She's like, nine. Please, just get online."

"Hang on," I said, putting my hand over the speaker. I whispered to Milo, "There's no computer in here."

Milo had figured out what was going on without me having to tell him. He'd seen this kind of thing play out before.

"Fake her."

"What?"

"She's lying. You should lie right back."

"No, no, that's not—she wouldn't do that."

Oh was yelling my name, her small voice desperate and haunted.

"You sure about this?" I asked Milo.

"No, but if I'm right, you're going to be glad you listened to me."

I breathed deep, filling my lungs with Captain Jack, and put the phone back to my ear.

"Jacob? Where are you?"

"I'm here, sorry, looking for a laptop here in the pipe shop. I'm at the coast with Milo. Um, it's going to take a second, but I can get online. Did you send me a picture or what?"

"I e-mailed it to you. Her name is Ann. I sent you her picture, you understand?"

"Of course I do."

"Just look at the picture and do your thing, okay? You can save her, Jacob. She needs us."

"Okay, I got it. Computer is up and we're online. Hang on."

I put my hand over the phone again and Milo broke in quietly.

"Where is she?"

"Don't know. She sounds sincere though, like she really needs me to do this."

"Did you do it? Did you do it?" Oh kept yelling into the phone.

"Okay, Oh, calm down. I see her. I see Ann."

"What are you waiting for? She's at the bottom of a well, Jacob. This kid could die any second. Do it!"

"Okay, okay — hang on."

I closed my eyes and thought of Oh's face. In my mind I saw her smiling, like she was when I met her, confident and full of life. It took me a second to go all the way through with it, because I was afraid of what might happen next.

I said the words out loud so Oh could hear them, and it wasn't two seconds later that she responded in a cold, detached voice.

"Thank you, Jacob. Good-bye."

The line went dead.

"There is no Ann," said Milo. "She's lying."

"I don't know — maybe...I just, damn! I hate this. If she was telling the truth, she'll never forgive me. She'll hate me for this."

Milo relit his pipe. There wasn't much else to say. I'd made a choice, and now we'd have to see how it turned out. I thought about calling or texting her, making sure she was okay, but I didn't have to. Not even a full minute had passed and she was already texting me.

You lied to me.

"Was I right?" Milo asked, leaning over so he could see the screen.

"Yeah, you were right."

Another text.

You killed that girl! You're a killer! Take it back!

"She's lying, Jacob. There is no girl. She wouldn't be telling you to take it back if there was. She's confused."

"What does this even mean?" I asked. But I knew what it meant. Oh had tried to take her own life. How else would she know I'd lied to her?

I remembered the way she said, *Thank you, Jacob. Good-bye.* I imagined her shutting the phone off and then picking up a gun or slicing herself with a razor blade. She'd figured out the truth on her own.

"Oh *wants* to die," I said, trying to hold myself together.

"I think we should open that box," Milo said.

I'd dropped the key on the bar, and Milo picked it up and held it out to me.

"It's our best shot at some answers. Open it, then we'll go find her."

I put the key in and turned it. The lid didn't tilt up, it slid back, like pins had been holding it in place. The whole top came off in my hand. Inside were yellow pages of paper covered in perfect handwriting.

It started off with a bang.

My name is Jonathan Fielding and I was born on July 12, 1872, in New England. It is now exactly 100 years later (July 12, 1972), and it seems as a good a time as any to record what I know.

I preface this document (I expect it to be short), by mentioning that while I like a good breakfast, a full pipe, and the smell of the Pacific, I do not particularly enjoy writing. Expect the brevity of Hemingway delivered with none of his skills.

This is the telling of a curse, passed from one man to another, and I don't suppose anyone will believe me. All of what I am about to say is covered in the bad stink of a lie. Nothing about it can be true. The characters involved are in every way implausible: me, a fifty-four-year-old nothing of a man, and he, the greatest escape artist of them all. What passed between us, and what came after, is even harder to believe.

I will be judged a deceiver and a fool after I'm gone, but that will not change what happened to me. My promise is all I have to give, and for most, it won't be enough. My pledge is simply this:

You'll find no lies here.

In October of the year 1926 I attended a show at the Princess Theater in Montreal and had the good

fortune of being called to the stage by the great-
est escape artist and magician of them all, Harry
Houdini.

I realize we are already in dangerous territory.
Houdini, you ask? The Houdini? Frankly, I feel the
same sense of disbelief, but these are the facts of
what has happened to me, and yes, they begin with
the supernaturally gifted escapist whether I like it or
not. So as to minimize the fantastic nature of these
events, I will, henceforth, refer to him as Mr. H.

Mr. H brought me to the center of the stage,
looked me straight in the eye, and told me I was
indestructible. Then he set me on a flat table and
proceeded to skewer me with seven knives: one in
each leg, one in each arm, one in my heart, another
in my neck, and a final blade in one ear and out the
other.

I didn't feel a thing while they were going in or
coming out. When he had each of the blades out
I was stood upright, and someone held a balloon
behind my head. Mr. H took out a revolver, placed
it against my forehead, and shot a bullet through
my skull, popping the balloon on the other side.
The crowd erupted in applause, and Mr. H sent me
back to my seat with a pat on the shoulder.

After the show, I found a scrap of paper in my
pocket (I will tape it to the last sheet of this telling).
It instructed me to come to the back door of the

theater and ask for Mr. Lutz, which I did. This was a code, I soon found, because minutes later I was sitting alone with Mr. H in his dressing room, the door closed behind us.

He stared at me as I told him how much I'd enjoyed the show. He let me run on until I stopped. After a time of awkward silence he spoke.

"You have it now."

I did not understand what he meant. I thought I was part of an elaborate trick that would find its end soon enough. But as he went on, I assumed he was not well, so fantastic were the things he told me. Mr. H began to describe to me, in the most curious way, that he had passed a power to me that he had gotten many years before.

You may ask yourself, why did he choose to gift a middle-aged nobody such as myself? I've asked the same thing many times over the years, and really, there's only one possible answer. I believe it was a truly random selection, that there was something in his heart that told him to let fate take its course. In his mind, he was not the one to choose. Someone or something else was meant to choose for him.

This power had long been trapped in the world of magic, so said Mr. H, and previously had always passed to the greatest among them, always kept as a dark secret known only to a few. It was, as

Mr. H described it, the only true magic there ever was. All the rest was sleight of hand and distraction and trickery. But this one thing, it was real, it was true. And what was more, it was very much like a living thing. The Black Lion, he called it, and at the sound of those words I felt something stirring in my chest. Something wicked that hadn't been there before.

"You feel it, don't you?" he asked me, a look of longing appearing on his face. "You feel the Black Lion. It has ways of its own, you will find."

I will try my best to remember and retell as precisely as I can everything that he then told me about this "Black Lion." He tried to explain it like this:

Everything has its opposite. Good and evil, black and white, death and immortality. He described the last of these as a trick of the soul. The idea of death, for us, is terrible. Wouldn't we all agree immortality sounds more appealing? That is the trick, or so he said, for in reality it is death that is magnificent and immortality the greatest of all despairs. We only return home in death. Everything that comes before is a pilgrimage, but the journey that leads forever to nowhere is hopeless. It is the black lion, circling humanity in a relentless spiral.

Somewhere, some time, in the long dark halls of magic, the black lion was summoned by a great magician who coveted immortality. Mr. H always doubted that this man, if he was a man at all, had the slightest idea of what he was doing. There was an evil desire in his heart to live forever and have the dark arts at his disposal. And yet he must have stumbled into it, knew nothing of what he'd done, and left it hidden among a very few when he grew tired of the thrill. It wasn't until later, down through the ages, that its beastly nature was better understood.

The black lion had been tamed, as it were, no longer free to roam, but trapped in the soul of one man.

I questioned him then, because at this point I still had very little idea what it was he meant by all this talk of immortality and the beast. I call it the beast because I feared it from the start. The mere thought of a black lion with its claws and teeth tearing from within me frightened me half to death. And yet, at the time, I felt certain the trick was about to be played out. The lights would flutter and a conjuring of one sort or another would make its appearance.

But then Mr. H did the strangest thing. He removed the same revolver from his desk drawer, pointed it at me, and shot a bullet through my heart. The sound was stunning in the confined space and made him grab for his ears in shock. I felt the bullet, like a nudge against my skin, and thought I was about to die. Within seconds there was a knock and *yelling. Mr. H opened the door, subdued the growing crowd with lies about a trick he was experimenting with, and closed the door to the world outside. I sat stunned, searching my coat for blood and finding none, unable to speak.*

When the door was closed and I had checked about myself, I, too, thought I'd been tricked. I congratulated him, then warned that people of my age succumbed to heart attacks all the time from lesser acts of trickery. He had to stab me again, twice actually, before I began to believe what he'd done to me. I really was indestructible, as he'd said.

This was no trick.

After that his words became even stranger, layered with complexity and metaphor. He took out a tattered journal, papers falling to the floor as he opened it up, and he began sifting through his notes. He was slow about his business, fanning over diagrams of escape tricks yet to be unleashed on the world, searching for something. He came to a certain page, closed the journal, but held the page in question with his finger.

He told me what he knew to be true. There was no record, nothing to fall back on. Only what Mr. H had been told and what he'd figured out on his own.

"The black lion is immortality with a secret door. Under its watch, a man can live forever, but he can end his long and lonely life anytime he wants."

"What do you mean?" I asked.

"Pass the power to someone else, but then you must go. Protect others at your own peril."

I asked him what would happen if I told someone else they were indestructible but chose not to take it—and here he was quick to warn me of using that word, a word of consequence, he called it. The truth was, I didn't think I had the nerve to kill myself under any circumstances.

He seemed to read my mind, his voice becoming cold and icy there in the room.

"You're thinking about giving it to me now, aren't you? I can see it in your eyes. Trust me, that would be a very bad idea."

"Why? Why can't I get rid of it?"

"Well, you could. You just wouldn't like what I'd have to do to you. If you give it back I really will have to kill you. You really will feel the pain and fear and loathing of death. And then you'll come back to life."

"Come back?" I asked him. "What do you mean, come back?"

"I think you know exactly what I mean, Mr. Fielding."

I was completely baffled. Did he mean to kill me if I yelled the words at him? Did he actually think I'd come back to life if he did? It was insanity!

He went on, and I truly assumed I was talking to a lunatic.

"Don't give it away unless you're sure, and for God's sake, don't start trying to pass it around to save other lives in peril. You're protected, it's as simple as that. You're its home now. Try to send the lion to an unrightful owner to save him from death, and darkness will descend. A life will be taken for every life saved, I tell you. Pass it around, and those you protect really will be cursed."

"I'm already cursed, you madman!" I screamed.

Mr. H looked at me with a stare that indicated he feared he'd chosen badly, as if he worried I was going to fail him. But he was wrong about me. My cowardice would prove helpful. The black lion has slept well for a hundred years. He'll sleep a thousand more before I'm through. I'm not going anywhere.

After a long pause of thoughtful reflection, Mr. H opened the journal he'd been holding and flopped it open in my direction.

"This is the Isengrim," said he. What new madness was this?

"If you make some mistakes...you'll need to contain the damage."

"Good Lord," I said. "What on earth are you talking about?"

He tore the pages from the journal violently and threw them in my face. I glanced at the indecipherable drawings for what might be—I could only imagine—some sort of contraption of the devil.

"I've used the power to thrill the world. You have the unfortunate appearance of a cowardly fool! What was I thinking?"

"Yes, by all means, what were you thinking? Take it back, you monster!"

A hundred years later, I can still see his eyes, so very tired. Looking back now, I see that he nearly did ask for it back. How many times had he cheated death over the years with every manner of elaborate escape?

I've kept the drawings for the Isengrim, his greatest escape trick never performed. I've even had it built, God knows why. What possible use could it have?

Unfortunately I never had a chance to ask Mr. H myself. He raced on to the Garrick Theatre in Detroit, where he performed his last show.

A week later Houdini was dead.

His last words, or so I was told by those who would know, were harrowing.

"And in my dream I saw a black lion of death coming to take me away."

This is the end of what I know. I have been careful. I have not let the black lion out. He is quiet, mostly, these many years. I often wonder if I dreamed the whole thing. I have only one worry in life, and it keeps me mostly to myself.

Will I ever say those words, and let the black lion out?

I didn't even realize I'd been standing the whole time I read until the weight of the message hit me and I slumped onto a stool at the bar. I sat there, numb to the world, as I thought about the horrible mistakes we'd made.

"This explains a lot," said Milo, and for once he wasn't trying to be funny to lighten my mood.

"Like what?" I said. I had a lot of ideas of my own, but two words were all I could get out of my mouth while my head was spinning with revelations.

"Well, for one thing, he didn't mean to curse you. Think about it. A car crash with you and him? It's like a once-in-a-hundred-years scenario. There's no way he even thought about what he was saying. It was a split-second decision. If he doesn't say those words, you die. He couldn't help himself."

"Yeah, I think you're right about that. Either that or the black lion saw its chance to get out and took it."

"Surprising how easy it is to sound like a nut case," Milo muttered.

I nodded. "Did I really just say that?" I shook my head, then thought again of Oh. Houdini's words, "darkness will descend," echoed in my mind. And I knew we didn't have much time to figure out a plan.

The plans for the Isengrim weren't in the stack of papers, but then I remembered that they were in one of the drawers of the Isengrim. We couldn't quite figure out how Mr. Coffin got the box or if he'd ever seen Mr. Fielding's letter, but we were starting to piece together some other things.

"I know what the Isengrim is for," said Milo. "I get it now."

"Really?"

"Yeah, really. If you're going to have to kill someone more than once, you'd need a controlled situation. The victim would need to be strapped down so they couldn't get away. You wouldn't want to risk a lot of blood everywhere if something went wrong, stuff like that. Who knows what a person acts like when they wake up from the dead. Could be bad."

"You're not thinking what I think you are—"

"Mr. Fielding never got himself into the situation we're in. If he had, he might understand it better. We were pretty close on the drive up here, but we were missing one important part."

"What part? I don't see it."

"The part where we bring Oh back."

Milo set the pipe in the corner of his mouth again, looking like a detective about to solve a crime, and it dawned on me what he meant.

"You're not serious?"

"I'm serious. She's like Mr. Fielding in the letter, when Houdini was still alive. You gotta read between the lines.

If Fielding would have given the power back then he'd have been just like Oh. He'd have been the dumping ground, like we talked about on the ride up here. Houdini gives him the power, but if he gets it back, then the trouble starts."

"I think I'm following," I said, "but I'm not sure."

"Jacob, what if the power gets confused? What if it's like there are two homes for it now: the one it clings to, Houdini, and the one it leaves behind, Mr. Fielding? Let's say Houdini does what we've done and gives the power to a *third* person in order to save them. Now the power has collected death, but it doesn't leave it with Houdini."

"Oh my God," I mumbled. "It waits."

"Yeah, it waits."

My mind was racing from one horrible thought to another. *I didn't follow the rules. When I gave Oh the power I should have died, but I didn't. She was the first person I gave it to. She was supposed to be its next home. I screwed up.*

It was all becoming clear, too clear, as I told Milo what I was thinking.

"The power waits until Houdini gives it back to Mr. Fielding."

"And then the power dumps the death."

I could barely breathe as I thought about what this would mean. Oh was the first person I'd passed the power to after Mr. Fielding died. I took it back. I gave it to another. I gave it to Oh again. And I'd done this how many times?

"We have to get them out of her," I said, terrified by what this simple statement could lead to. "But how?"

Milo had a look of certainty on his face I wasn't ready to share.

"I'm guessing we'll have to kill them out of her."

I was horrified by the idea, but I could only put up half a fight. Something rang true about what Milo was proposing.

"That is *so* crazy," I said. "It can't be right."

"More like it *has* to be right. It explains everything. And if there's a whole bunch of deaths piled up inside Oh, then it stands to reason: Killing Oh the same number of times is the only way to get them out."

"Listen to yourself, Milo. You've gone insane!"

"No, I haven't. You know I'm right."

Deep down, between the facts we could see and the letter we'd just read, it was starting to sound possible.

"Only one problem," said Milo.

"We don't know how many deaths Oh...," I started, trying to find the words, "...*collected* along the way."

"One thing's for sure. It's a lot. Which is probably why she's turned into a zombie."

My phone vibrated unexpectedly and I grabbed it off the bar.

"It's her, isn't it?" asked Milo.

It was annoying how frequently Milo was right.

I'm ready to talk. can I see you?

"Ask her where she is," said Milo, so I did. We started

for the door and ended up in the car, driving down High-
way 99 before she answered.

Meet at dark. holy cross parking lot.

"We can make it back easy by four and three quarters,"
said Milo, racing away from Lincoln City. "Gets dark
around five. We're good."

I texted her back, told her we'd be there, while Milo punched
in "Black Dog" on his iPod and set the volume to ten.

Time to think.

SEVEN HOURS TO MIDNIGHT

5:05 PM

We rolled into the Holy Cross driveway and it was already dark, a damp layer of frigid fog cutting our visibility to about ten feet. It had been that way since the sun started setting at around 4:30, cutting our speed in half for the last ten miles into town.

"God, it gets dark early," said Milo, trying to defuse the tension. "We need to move to California."

"She won't answer," I said, tapping out another text in an endless stream of attempts I'd made to reach Oh since leaving the coast.

"Well, we're here now. The question is what to do once we find her."

We'd talked endlessly about this on the way and agreed we basically had no idea. If I took the power from her, she might try to kill herself. Obviously she was so full of dark-ness she'd lost any ability to think rationally. Death for Oh, and I mean the real deal, was the only thing we figured she thought about. Then there was the other option—letting her keep the power—but that made us both pretty ner-vous. What if she turned her wrath on us?

When we reached the end of the long driveway and passed into the parking lot, our headlights shot through the soupy fog to the edge of the woods. Milo parked the car and I thought about all the kids who'd been scared by the stories that were told about escapees from the mental hospital. It occurred to me that now there might actually be a sort of monster with sunken eyes out there, unkillable. No one would think for a minute that she was dangerous—until it would be too late.

"We have to find her," I said. Something about the way those words sounded on my lips made me choke up. She wasn't a monster, she was Ophelia James. She was beautiful and perfect. I missed her.

"Should we lock the doors?" asked Milo. He craned his neck and looked up into the cloud of fog. Somewhere up there was the top of the five-story school with its flat roof. I knew it was flat because I'd been up there before, watching Milo throw rolls of toilet paper into the open courtyard as a prank. I remember it seemed really high and I wanted to get down.

My phone buzzed to life and the screen went blue and was glowing in my hand.

Miss me? I bet you did.

"Something's not right," I whispered.

Take it back.

Milo reached around and locked his door. By the time his hand was back on the steering wheel, I'd begun typing out a response:

Where are you? we're her

Just as I was putting my thumb on the *e* to finish my note, something huge and heavy hit the top of Milo's car. The roof buckled over our heads and slammed my head against the cracked dashboard. Glass flew everywhere from the blown windows; the windshield spidered and popped.

First we screamed, then we were both still as statues, the only sound our breathing and the clunking whirl of Milo's engine.

"It's her," Milo whispered, his words coming in waves between choppy breaths. "Has to be."

I wouldn't have believed it if I didn't hear her moving up there, then see her feet land on the hood of the car. She crawled down to the pavement and stood in the headlights, staring at us.

She'd changed since I'd seen her choking Ethan half to death. The fog ran thick and wispy through the headlights, casting a gloomy spotlight across Oh's body. The color had gone completely out of her face and her eyes were vacant. It didn't look like Oh anymore. It was like a corpse of Oh. But a determined one. Her face was charged with a desire to kill or destroy.

She began to move, which startled me so much I lurched back and hit my head on the caved roof of the car. I didn't realize it until then, but I had been crouched low in my seat, peering over the dashboard like a hunted animal.

Oh put her hands on the hood of the car and it looked like she was about to crawl forward to the splintered windshield.

"Don't take it back," said Milo, stepping on the gas and blasting gravel.

"Milo, NO!" I screamed as I heard the awful thud of Oh's legs being hit.

Oh bounced off what was left of the windshield and flew forward, crashing on the sidewalk leading into the school. The crash with Mr. Fielding played through my head: the blood, his broken body, the smell of burning rubber.

I put my head out the window and yelled Oh's name as she rolled to a stop, took out her phone as if nothing had happened, and started typing out a message.

"Go back!" I screamed, unable to even see Milo's face between the crushed sections of the roof.

"Hell with that. She's fine. It's us I'm worried about."

By the time we reached the end of the drive, my phone was buzzing from the floorboard, and I saw the soft light glow. I picked it up, imagining her walking through the fog and into the woods.

You should have taken it back. now it's too late.

"What'd she say?" asked Milo as we tore out of the driveway onto Haysville Boulevard, fishtailing on the slick pavement.

"She's gone, Milo. I mean really gone. What are we going to do?"

◆ ◆ ◆

We stopped a mile later in a public park that was closed for the night, and Milo cracked open the trunk of his car.

"Man, she really did a number on this thing," he said, slamming the trunk shut and carrying a heavy metal tool-box. Duct tape, a hacksaw, hammers, a crowbar, these were always on hand in a junker like Milo's. He went to work on the splayed windshield first, busting it out with a hammer and a pair of Vise-Grips.

"I'm calling Father Tim," I said.

"Why would you want to do that?" asked Milo, taking the hammer in hand. "He's not going to understand this."

I wasn't searching for help so much as comfort. I couldn't tell Father Tim what was really going on, but I needed to talk to someone solid, someone with a voice of reason who could make the world feel halfway normal again.

I heard Milo start banging away on the inside of the roof of his car and walked deeper into the abandoned park where I could be alone. The fog was so thick it made my hair wet and my phone slick in my hand.

Father Frank picked up at the church house. Great.

"Is Father Tim there? It's Jacob."

"He's here, where are you? I made a roast and some beans and potatoes if you're hungry. Leftovers are in the fridge, middle shelf, in that white round Tupperware, you know the one…"

"Father Frank, listen, I really need to talk to Father Tim if you could find him."

He made a wheezing sound, like I'd hurt his feelings, and dropped the phone on the counter. I could hear *Jeopardy!* in the background, which the old guys liked to watch during the time of year when night came early.

"Jacob, that you?" asked Father Tim.

"Yeah, we're back in town, beat the fog by a hair. I think I'll stay with Milo tonight if that's okay."

"Glad you made it. I was getting worried. By all means stay at Milo's — Father Frank cooked dinner."

I didn't say anything, just stared into the night of the park and looked at the fog getting thicker.

"Everything okay?" asked Father Tim.

"I think I have my answer," I said. "About whether or not there's a hell."

I'd thought a lot about Father Tim's class on the drive home. Reading Mr. Fielding's letter had put things in a whole new light.

"I think you're wrong, Father Tim. There's a hell all right. It's just not where people say it is."

"Interesting. Where do you think it is?"

"It's here. It's life, or it's what we turn life into, I guess. It's like we have to pass through all this painful stuff to get to where we're supposed to be, on the other side."

"You sure you don't want to come home tonight?" asked Father Tim.

"What if I couldn't get home?" I started to tear up, working hard to keep it together. "What if I were stuck here forever?"

"Well, for starters, that's impossible. But if it were something that could actually happen, then you're probably right. You'd be lost, separated from God forever. I could see where that might be unpleasant."

"I gotta go."

"I can come get you if you want."

"No, I'm good—I'll be back in the morning. I'll clean my room."

The park was starting to feel like a bad idea as I ended the call, like Oh might drop out of a tree any moment and try to tear my arms off.

I heard a branch move in the wind and just about jumped out of my pants, then made a beeline for Milo. He'd already slid back into his seat and started the car up again. It didn't look too bad, the roof was higher than it was, but it was going to be rough driving around without a windshield. The heater was on full blast from the dashboard, creating a wet, warm, cold mix of swirling air as we pulled out from under the trees.

"I kept the tools in the backseat," said Milo. "In case we need to protect ourselves."

I sat there, thinking about what it would be like to hit

Oh with a hammer, and hoped to God it wouldn't come to that.

By 10:30 we'd tried texting or calling Oh a hundred times but she wouldn't answer. We'd sat at cafés warming up, we'd sat in the loft trying to figure out where else to look, we'd driven for hours in the freezing fog.

At 11:00 we drove by the woods behind Holy Cross. We yelled her name, listening for movement, but with the fog and the deep night setting in, we couldn't bring ourselves to get out of the car and hike into the gloom.

At around 11:30 we went to Oh's apartment for the third time, too afraid to knock on the door. If Oh was in there with her mom, at least she was safe. But we were pretty sure Oh had fed her mom a line about staying at a friend's house.

"She's still got it, right?" asked Milo.

It was nearly midnight, and it was maybe the tenth time Milo had asked me. It was cool, I guess, because it meant he really cared about her. He didn't want her dead anymore than I did.

Come on, Oh, just answer me. Please.

I thought of her smile and her blond bangs hanging just over her eyes and said the words again, just to be sure.

You are indestructible.

A few minutes later, driving through the Holy Cross neighborhood and feeling desperate, my phone vibrated three times in my hand and the screen flashed blue. Milo slammed on the brakes and pulled to the curb, leaning over the gear shift to see what it was.

Call me.

"Maybe she's finally ready to talk," said Milo. "Where do you think she is?"

Between the cold and my nerves, my hands were shaking so badly I speed-dialed the wrong number. Father Frank answered, and I had a momentary horror-filled moment when I thought it was Oh, her voice mangled into something unspeakable.

I hung up on the old priest and tried again. It rang three times. When Oh answered on the other end of the line, she didn't say anything. I could hear her breathing and imagined the way her nose was moving as the air went in and out.

"Where are you?" I asked.

"You know the place," she whispered.

"Oh, please. Just tell me where you are."

"You can't make me keep it."

"Where are you?"

"Take it back and I'll tell you," she said. There was a desperate cunning in her voice.

"I can't take it back," I said. "Not yet."

"Then we've got nothing to talk about."

There was a short pause in which I said her name, but she didn't answer.

Then I heard her screaming. It was a different kind of scream, her voice ruptured and jumpy, as if she were bouncing down an endless flight of stairs.

"Turn the car around," I said. "I know where she is."

MIDNIGHT

The clock turned to midnight as Milo parked the car and we walked up the sidewalk.

"I don't see why you're so sure about this," he said without the slightest effort at keeping his voice down. We crept up near the door and found it was locked.

"She's in there," I said.

My phone vibrated in my pocket and I pulled it out.

I HATE YOU. TAKE IT BACK

"Come on," I said, typing in the word *NO* as I took off at a run.

The street grew darker, only one lamp overhead in a foggy layer of sky.

About six feet up, against the brick wall of the building, there was a broken window. Underneath sat a folding metal chair, the kind we used at assemblies. I collapsed the chair and looked at the bottom, found the paint-stenciled words HOLY CROSS.

"I don't think it's Father Tim in there," I said.

"Okay, now I believe you." said Milo. "Come on."

We ran back in the direction from which we'd come. Milo took his ring of car keys out of his pocket and found the one he needed, turning the dead bolt on the front door.

"Hang on," he said, bolting for his car and reaching into the backseat. When he emerged again, he had the hammer and a long metal chisel. He leaned back in, grabbed the roll of duct tape and showed it to me, but I waved it off. I got the chisel, which felt more like a knife in my hand than I was comfortable with.

Milo opened the door slowly, noiselessly, and we both stepped inside. When the door was closed again, there was only one source of light in the room. It was a thin shaft way off in the corner, and we silently made our way to its source, the old wooden floor creaking softly under our feet.

"You got a plan, right?" asked Milo.

"Not really."

"We need to get her calmed down, explain things to her."

I knew in my heart that wasn't going to work. And I'd lied, I did have a plan. I just didn't want to talk about it.

"You think you could go through with it?" asked Milo.

"Go through with what?"

"You know what I mean. Could you kill her? Could you do it if it saved her life?"

It sounded so twisted: *Kill the one I love to save her.* It made no sense. And it was so much worse with Oh, because who knew how many deaths we'd piled up inside her? Even if what we were planning to do worked, even if I could do it and she came back, it wouldn't matter. I'd have to get them all out. And the scariest part? One too many kills and she really would be dead.

My phone vibrated in my pocket and I stopped, staring down at the message.

I know you're here.

"She's down there," I said. "She's been using the Isengrim."

"*What?* No way," said Milo.

I thought of the horrible sounds she'd made when she called, and I could almost see the electricity charging through her.

"When we get down there," whispered Milo, "go straight for the shelves to your left. That's where the best weapons are."

I looked at him in the dark, still not believing the fact that it might go that far.

"Dude, she's *indestructible*," he reminded me. "We have to protect ourselves or she'll kill us both." He held up the hammer. "I'd rather have a mace if I can get my hands on one."

Milo disappeared into the darkness of Coffin Books, leaving me alone and staring at the shaft of light leading into the basement. When he returned, he was carrying a baseball bat.

"You want the hammer?" he asked, holding it out to me. "I like my chances better with this thing."

I took the hammer in my free hand, and we crept closer to the shelf that had been pushed aside, listening for movement from below. The electric sound of the Isengrim echoed up the stairwell.

I crept down the stairs with Milo right behind me until I was close enough to see. I couldn't take that last step. I couldn't see Oh that way, convulsing, dying but not dying. A second later I heard Oh hit the floor like a sack of flour.

"Be careful," said Milo, his voice cracking with fear as he crossed to the shelves of weapons. "Remember, she's not dead. She's coming back."

I stepped the rest of the way into the basement and felt warm air lingering with cold earth. Oh was lying on her side, her back to me, and she almost looked like a normal girl again. It was like she was sleeping, all curled up in the fetal position in her jeans and black T-shirt.

But then she moved, not slowly like I'd expected, as if she were coming awake. She was up on her feet all at once, pulling the pink notebook out of her pocket and slapping it down on the metal surface of the Isengrim. She went to work scrawling something out with a half-melted ballpoint pen.

"Here," Milo whispered. He was trying to hand me the bat, because he'd picked up a mace off the shelf. The surface of the ball was covered in rusted nails, and Milo dangled the foot-long chain from his hand.

"That bat won't do you any good," said Oh. Her voice

startled both of us. She was sitting on the Isengrim, staring at us. "Hit me with it all you want."

"Give me the notebook," I said. It was the only thing that mattered, because the answers I needed were hidden in there.

"Come and take it from me."

"I need to see the notebook."

She walked a couple of steps toward us.

"Take back the power and I'll give it to you."

"You know I can't do that."

"I think you can."

Without any warning, she leaped wildly in my direction, her body against mine with such speed and force I didn't have time to lift the hammer and beat her back. I stumbled, fell backward, and felt Oh's weight pinning me down against the floor.

"Take it back or I'll kill you."

"What should I do?" yelled Milo.

Oh had one hand on my neck and the other on her heart, which was where I'd planted my fist trying to hold her back. The handle of the chisel was in my balled up fist, but the long thin rod was somewhere inside Oh. I couldn't believe what I'd done, couldn't imagine I was capable...

"That felt good. Will you do it again?"

Oh yanked my hand away, pulling seven or eight inches of long, thin metal slowly free from her flesh. The expression on her face was almost euphoric, like a black adrenaline rush was blasting through her veins.

"Kill! Kill! Kill!" she laughed.

The chisel was turned on me now, both of us holding it together.

"Oh, please, listen to me," I pleaded. "I'm sorry. I can fix this. I can still protect you."

There was a small look of recognition then, like some deep part of the real girl I loved was in there, hearing my voice, believing I could take it away.

And then Milo swung the mace hard and fast without any warning. It came under her body, caught her in the chest, and lifted her off her feet, sending her careening through the air.

"Milo, NO!" I couldn't stand the thought of rusted nails cutting through her skin, but they had, ripping the handle out of Milo's hand as Oh crashed on the dirt floor of the basement.

Oh sat up, looked at her chest, touched it. She took the pink notebook and the pen out of her hip pocket, flipping drunkenly to the right page. She scrawled another cross, and then another. We'd killed her twice in the span of about a minute and it made me feel like throwing up.

Oh put the notebook and the pen in her pocket again, and when she looked up at me, she was crying. She got up on her feet and lifted herself up on the Isengrim, wrapping the bare wires around her wrist. She hadn't figured out how to put the Isengrim back together so it would work the way it was designed to, but she'd come up with her own twisted version that appeared to work just fine.

"You did this to me," she sobbed. "You made me this way."

"It's a trick," whispered Milo. "Don't get near her."

Oh grabbed the lever with the fingers of her broken arm and drew it toward her, sending a wave of electricity up the line and into her arm. She convulsed grotesquely, screaming into the open air of the basement. It was harrowing, the way her hair lifted off her head and her eyes darted in every direction. She was the closest thing I'd ever seen to a monster, lost in some unfathomable torture she couldn't stop inflicting on herself.

And in my dream I saw a black lion of death coming to take me away.

I swear I saw it then, rising over Oh, gripping her head in its black claws.

"Please, Oh," I whispered. I knew she couldn't hear me, but I wished she could. The hum of electric power scorching through her veins must have sounded like a freight train. I stepped closer to her, the tears starting to come.

"Stay back, Jacob!" yelled Milo.

But I kept going, one slow step at a time.

"I need the pink notebook, Oh. Will you give it to me?"

She slammed the lever down on the Isengrim and went limp for an instant, then lifted her head and stared at me through shimmering eyes.

"I didn't want to start a fire," she said.

I had wondered, but hearing her say it broke my heart.

"No one got hurt," I said. "And it wasn't your fault. It was mine."

She started crying again, softer this time.

"I didn't want to kill Ethan," she said.

Oh had thought she'd taken the life of an innocent person.

"You didn't," I told her. "He's fine, honest."

"Jacob, use your head," Milo said from behind me. "She's trying to trick you. Don't get any closer!"

Oh reached into her back pocket and pulled out the pink notebook. She flipped it open to the page full of crude crosses. I was nearly sick when I saw how many there were.

"Oh God, you didn't."

Her pen lay on the surface of the Isengrim with its plastic shell melted and deformed. She picked it up and put another cross on the page.

"You were supposed to protect me," she said, dropping the pen on the metal slab of the Isengrim. "I trusted you."

She touched the pink cast, battered and broken, where I'd written the words. She'd added diamonds of different sizes, all of them filled in black.

"I didn't know what I was doing, but I do now," I explained, taking one more step toward her. Her fingers darted to the handle.

"Just take it back, Jacob."

I took the last step, close enough to reach out and put my hand on her face.

"Jacob, don't!" yelled Milo.

I touched Oh's face, felt the coldness of her skin. There was no Isengrim, no electricity, no Milo or Mr. Fielding. Just her pleading eyes staring back at me.

"I'm sorry," she said, pulling the handle slowly toward her. I felt the first jolt come through her face and into the palm of my hand.

"I love you, Ophelia James."

When I pulled my hand away, she was gone. The power was mine again, whispered in the quiet of my own head. I'd finally taken it back. I took her hand in my own, pushed the handle down again, and felt her body fall limp in my arms.

Ophelia James was dead.

◆　◆　◆

She was lighter than I expected when I picked her up. Or maybe it was having the power back inside me, giving me strength I hadn't known for a while. I laid her on the Isengrim and listened, hoping for sounds of life.

"What if we were wrong, what then?" I asked Milo. He was standing at the far end of the Isengrim holding the bat, looking at Oh's shoes.

"The rubber's melted on her Cons."

He couldn't answer me or didn't want to. Either I'd just killed Oh or she'd come back to life at some point. It could be ten seconds, ten minutes, ten hours—we had no idea if she'd ever return.

285

"What if she doesn't come back?"

I was looking at Oh's face, getting lost in the dread of what I'd done.

"We should strap her down, before it's too late," Milo said.

"She's not coming back."

He cracked the bat against the surface of the Isengrim and I snapped to attention.

"Stop it, Jacob. She's in there, you know she is. And if we're right, then there's a lot more killing to be done. Unless you want to chase her around the basement all night we need to strap her down."

Milo set the bat on top of the Isengrim and went to work on the straps at Oh's feet. I took one of Oh's cold wrists in my hand, the one without the pink cast, and fumbled around with the leather strap designed to hold her down. I was facing Milo, really having to concentrate to get the strap on tight. I glanced up at Milo, down at Oh's feet, and he looked at me. The expression on his face was like he'd seen a ghost, and he scrambled for the bat.

He told me later she was starting to sit up behind me, staring at the back of my head.

I turned just in time to see Oh's pink cast windmilling toward my face. She put everything she had into it, catching me square in the nose with the words I'd written thirteen days before.

I felt the blow, felt it when my head hit the hard dirt floor and my neck twisted inhumanly.

When I looked up, blood was dripping out of Ophelia's nose as she worked the leather strap on her wrist with her one free hand.

"Jacob! You have to do it again!" cried Milo. He held the bat, but I could see he really didn't want to use it. Oh wasn't indestructible anymore. If he hit her with a baseball bat, bones were really going to break. We couldn't go that route no matter what happened.

"Get me off this thing!" screamed Oh. "Murderer!"

She kept screaming that word, free of the wrist shackle and down to her feet, trying desperately to get free. The wires had flown off her hands and dangled near the floor, and I took them in my hand.

"Oh, listen to me," I said, trying to stay calm as she swung her arms to keep me away. "I'm trying to save you."

"Give it back. Please, Jacob, give it back to me."

She was pleading as I got up on the table and lay down next to her. She kept hitting me with that cast, crying out for me to give her the power back. I wrapped my body around hers, held her tighter than I've ever held anyone before, and asked Milo to pull the lever.

We were fused together, me and Oh, the same electricity coursing through our veins. It was beautiful and terrible, because I didn't feel any pain at all, just the sweet feeling of holding the girl I loved as she passed from life to death. Milo cut the charge, and Oh lay dead in my arms.

I wept openly then, unable to hold back what it felt like

to see Oh die not once, but twice. And more than that. Laying on the Isengrim, my face buried in her hair, I couldn't stand that I'd been the one to kill her.

"I'm sorry," said Milo, touching me on the back. "I'll do the rest if you want."

He peeled me off of Oh and held me by my shoulders.

"We're going to get through this. She's coming back."

I needed to hear those words, to think this madness had the possibility of success. This time, we wasted no time getting Oh completely strapped down.

"Where's the notebook?" asked Milo.

"Back pocket," I answered, taking it in my hand. I handed it to Milo and he flipped to the page where Oh had kept track of every life we'd saved. Every one had a cross, carefully drawn and perfect. On the opposite page there were more crosses, but they weren't lovingly rendered. They were scrawled, crooked, and wild. There were more of these, and we knew what they were.

They were all the times Oh had tried to kill herself.

◆　◆　◆

"She can never know what she's done. We can't let that happen."

"This is the sickest thing ever," said Milo. He was holding the pink notebook, where we'd crossed out all but two of the twenty-seven crosses.

288

"She's coming to," I said.

Oh was lying flat on top of the Isengrim, her ankles and arms in the shackles. "Where am I? What's happening?" she said, pulling on the shackles and wincing in pain.

"What are you doing to me?" she said, panic rising in her voice as she realized where she was. It was like her memory was shattered. I couldn't stand to see her this way, frightened beyond words.

"Try to stay still. We had to take your cast off," I said. Her arm wouldn't stay locked in place very well with the cast on, so we'd removed it. It had slid off with surprising ease, and we soon realized it had been taken off before.

Under the cast, in the middle of her forearm, Oh had gotten a tattoo. It must have burned and itched without relief for days. There wasn't much to it, just a simple black diamond with a bright pink center.

I pulled the handle down and had the horrifying experience of watching my girlfriend convulse before my eyes again. Ten seconds later I pulled the handle back, and she was gone.

Milo swirled black marks through another cross in the notebook. There was only one left. "Are you worried about getting it wrong?" asked Milo.

I didn't answer him. Of course I was worried. I wasn't certain she'd written them *all* down. What if one cross had been missed? Some of the crosses had notations next to them, so I knew they were accounted for.

+ *Girl on the water* + *Home run shot to the head* + *Off the roof* + *Fire*

"Oh," I whispered, drawing my hand over her hair. "Did you write one down that you shouldn't have? Did you know it would come to this? Did you plan for it? Please say no."

We sat in silence, waiting, not knowing if she would come back. When seven minutes passed, I got up and started pacing back and forth. Eight minutes, longer than before, and I was beside myself with worry. When it reached ten minutes, I began to feel my heart breaking. The times between had been getting progressively longer with every jolt, but there was no way to know for sure. Had we killed Ophelia James, or had we saved her?

"No more crosses," Milo mumbled.

"Let's get her out of here."

I unshackled Oh from the Isengrim and carried her up the stairs with help from Milo. I went to Mrs. Coffin's easy chair and sat down. Oh lay dead on my lap, and I touched the pink and black tattoo on her arm, wishing she could feel it.

"Get me the cast, will you?" I asked Milo.

I looked up at him, and he told me how long she'd been dead, his voice trembling and afraid.

"Fourteen minutes."

"Please, get the cast."

Milo backed up slowly until he reached the door to the basement, then he turned and was gone.

I wanted to be alone, to tell her how sorry I was and say good-bye. I thought of Mr. Fielding and what he'd said about the long walk all by himself. I didn't think I had the strength to go it alone, not for a hundred years, not even for a hundred seconds.

"I can't do this all by myself," I whispered.

I touched Oh's brow, kissed her on the lips, and felt a bloom of breath on my cheek.

Her eyes came open, slowly at first and then all at once. She yawned loudly and I heard Milo coming slowly up the stairs.

"Did you take advantage of me in my sleep?"

She pulled me into a bleary-eyed hug. I'm sure she would have said something else if Milo hadn't been dancing and howling in the middle of the room. When I finally got him calmed down, I reached out for the pink cast and he gave it back. I read the words but didn't say them out loud. Oh was never going to get the power from me again.

"We've got a few things to talk about," I said.

Oh closed her eyes, half asleep, drifting off.

"I'm so tired. Why does it smell like burnt rubber in here? Can we go to the beach tomorrow?"

"Yeah," I said. "We can go to the beach. Not tomorrow, but soon."

And then she smiled faintly and fell asleep in my arms.

ONE WEEK LATER

We did go back to the beach, and I got to do all the things I'd planned to do with Oh. We ate saltwater taffy, took turns on her longboard on the boardwalk, ate chowder, and walked along the beach. When night was about to fall, we made a fire and stared out at the ocean.

"What are you not telling me, Jacob Fielding?" she asked me. It had become a familiar question.

"Nothing," I said. "I've told you everything."

It's no good starting a relationship with a lie, but her memory had turned faulty and I couldn't tell her the whole truth. She remembered things—the fire, getting the tattoo, a lot of what we'd been through—but she had no memory of killing herself over and over again. No memory of having started the fire or almost killing Ethan. It was as if the most troubling events were covered in black tar and couldn't be seen. I worried it wouldn't always be like that. Someday, after the shock had worn off, she might remember some of what she'd done, and then she'd know I had lied to her.

But I was experienced at holding on to secrets, and Milo had promised me he wouldn't tell Oh anything she couldn't remember on her own. It was a risk we were willing to take.

"He's crazy to let you take his car this far away," she said, smiling into a soft wind that curled her hair back.

"I agree."

I'd told her about the money and the truth about the accident with Mr. Fielding. She hadn't hated me like I thought she might for driving Mr. Fielding into a tree. My best friend and the girl I loved didn't loathe me for my mistake, but I couldn't help hating myself. I hoped it would go away in time, but I had my doubts.

"So you're sure about this?" she asked me, poking a stick in the fire, moving hot coals against the sand.

"I'm sure."

"Not even once in a while?"

"Never again, and that's my final answer."

I had told her my days of slipping people the diamond were over. If we were going to do any good in the future, it would have to come from me keeping the power to myself.

293

She had no way of knowing why, and I had a feeling it would be a wedge between us. Only Milo and I knew the truth, and that's the way I planned to keep it.

I sat there thinking about Father Tim and Mr. Coffin. I think they were near enough to Mr. Fielding before and to me now to feel the power of a hidden thing. I think they have this feeling still, a sense that just around the corner of what they can see there lies a dark secret. I don't plan to tell either one of them, *ever*, but I have a feeling they will hover around me, searching for clues, untill they grow old and weary with age.

I put my arm around Oh and pulled her close. She cared more about the world than I did, and I wished Mr. Fielding had given the power to her instead of me. She would have done a lot of good with it. She and the black lion would have gotten along swimmingly, but me? I just wished it would go away. I wished it would die and never come back.

My phone buzzed in the pocket of my hoodie and Oh fished it out, holding the screen where we could both see it.

Taking a few swings at the batting cages. set to slow pitch. i'm killing it!

"He's so lying," Oh joked. "Milo couldn't hit a baseball off a tee."

I stared off into the sunset and leaned my head against Oh's, running my fingers along the edge of the pink diamond on her arm.

"I sort of feel like hitting a baseball," said Oh, staring up into my eyes. "You?"

"They close at nine," I said, glancing at my watch. "If we hurry we can make it."

A hundred years from now I'm sure I'll feel differently, when Oh and Milo are gone and I'm left to march into Mr. Fielding's arms alone. I can already see myself in the distant future, standing behind the counter at Sir Walter Raleigh's, sending smoke signals out into the world in search of a conversation.

"Great to be alive, isn't it?" asked Oh, wrapping her arms around my neck. She looked amazing.

"Yeah, it is great," I agreed.

My long journey hadn't turned lonely yet, but I had the feeling, there on the beach, that the best time would fly by almost unnoticed. Like the one or five or ten minutes parked on the side of the road on the way to the Enchanted Forest, all good time would pass me by.

"Race you to the clunker," said Oh.

And then she was running, kicking up sand and calling for me to follow.

I felt the distance between her and my long walk alone grow a little shorter.

◆ ◆ ◆

If you could have one superpower, what would it be?

I still ask people that question all the time, and I get the same kind of answers I've always gotten. Flying. Reading minds. Walking through walls.

I've finally settled on the one I want, and it sure isn't the one I got. It's simple, really, something everyone else has that I don't. I can walk into a burning building, dive off a bridge, get hit by a bus, or drive a car into a tree doing ninety. I'd give it all up in a heartbeat for the one thing I can't have.

All I really want is to stay with my friends all the way to the end.

The power to never be alone is the only answer there is for a guy like me.